MÁRQUEZ EMS GULAM *& Others*

Celebrating
30 Years of Publishing
in India

MÁRQUEZ EMS GULAM

& Others

SELECTED SHORT STORIES

BENYAMIN

TRANSLATED FROM THE MALAYALAM BY

SWARUP B.R.

HARPERPERENNIAL

An Imprint of HarperCollins *Publishers*

First published in English in India by Harper Perennial 2023
An imprint of HarperCollins *Publishers*
4th Floor, Tower A, Building No. 10, Phase II, DLF Cyber City,
Gurugram, Haryana – 122002
www.harpercollins.co.in

2 4 6 8 10 9 7 5 3 1

P-ISBN: 978-93-5629-567-4
E-ISBN: 978-93-5629-568-1

Typeset in 11.5/15.7 Adobe Caslon Pro at
Manipal Technologies Limited, Manipal

Printed and bound at
Thomson Press (India) Ltd

Contents

Author's Note

STORIES CANNOT BE PULLED OUT of thin air like magicians and sanyasis pull out vibhuti. They are deeply rooted in life.

It is a quarter century since I started writing. Though I stepped into the literary world as a short-story writer, short stories account for only a small percentage of what I have written till date. I have spent most of my energy, time, imagination and craft on novels, travelogues and essays. I have often thought about why it transpired thus – that, too, in spite of the fact that I am an ardent fan of short stories. One reason could be the fear that I would not be able to do justice to the intense experience that the short story is. It could be because I've always felt that the novel is a more flexible medium. It could also perhaps be that most of the stories that have taken shape in my mind could not have been contained using this form. Be that as it may, I consider it a great blessing that short stories come in search of me at regular intervals. Yes. It would be truer to say that stories come in search of me rather than say that I venture forth in search of them. Most of the short stories that I have written are those that landed right in front of me, as though they were destined to be written by me. Why, I have even asked some of them why they could not have dropped in on another writer.

My stories are not far removed from life. Though imagination, like leaves, has sprouted, the roots remain firmly entrenched in the soil of life. I do not have the skill to create stories from empty, imaginary mindscapes. My stories spring only from life experiences. Which is why I said that my stories most often come in search of me. To be more precise, the people, the experiences and the situations come in search of me.

It was while we were sitting in a wayside café in the old souk of Doha, sipping Sulaimani tea and smoking hookah, that a friend narrated the story of a private zoo that once existed within the city from where the animals escaped one day and how one man kept searching for them tirelessly. It was at the same time, coincidentally, that we heard the news of how the Lebanese prime minister had resigned when he was in Saudi Arabia. It was at that moment that the story 'Gulam Hussain' was born.

It was whilst on a journey through various villages from Pune to Varanasi with two friends that the two stories 'Solapur' and 'Bukkaram's Son' came to me. In fact, 'Bukkaram's Son' was written as a sequel to 'When the Clocks Stopped', a story written twenty-five years ago by the famous Malayalam writer Subhash Chandran, in the backdrop of the Latur earthquake. He tells the story of

Bukkaram, the protagonist, who was stealing a clock while the earthquake was happening. I tell the story of how a quarter century later, Bukkaram's son, caught in the same circumstances, continues to be a thief. This story was also inspired by the experiences people shared when we visited the 'Village of Thieves' in Maharashtra.

The Kashmiri doctor I met when I was working in Bahrain, who narrated his experiences right through a night of ghazals and whisky, inspired the story 'Javed the Mujahideen'. The experience shared by a Brazilian girl whom I met during my trip to Ireland inspired 'Alice in Wonderland'. It was from Gazan, the guide on our pilgrimage to Jerusalem, that I got 'The Stones of Gazan'. The experiences I had during the eleven years that I spent working in an American military base led to 'Two Soldiers in Yet Another Arabian Tale', 'EMS and the Girl' and 'Addis Ababa'.

Thus, the path each story took to reach me is etched in my memory. However, rather than just narrate an experience, an incident or a life, it is when I can infuse my thoughts, my beliefs, my fears, my politics into these experiences, incidents and lives, that I get into a story. Because I believe that in this day and age, stories are not read merely out of curiosity – they have a mission to fulfil.

In fact, many of these stories – 'The Stones of Gazan', 'Solapur', 'Javed the Mujahideen', 'Two Soldiers in Yet Another Arabian Tale' – are infused with the politics of love, brotherhood and humanity that I wish to share;

I have, however, taken great care to not let this affect the basic stories and your enjoyment of the same. What I present here for you is a collection of stories where I have managed to do this infusion, a collection of short stories that I believe are the most important ones in my literary life. I hope you will accept them, read them, and share your feedback.

Affectionately,
Benyamin
December 2022

Márquez

1

GREGORY GEORGE MATHEWS, THE YOUNG journalist, woke up one fine morning from a rather sweet dream, realized that he had transformed into none other than Márquez, and was lying on a bed in a hotel room in Mexico.

2

What invited the dream in which he was a dandelion wafting through the outskirts of Cartagena in Columbia on a Monday evening was probably the delightfully exhausted slumber that he had slipped into the previous day, after reading two books back to back: a spiritual-intellectual book that postulated that no soul ever leaves the earth – it just leaves one body to inhabit another – in fact, the soul might keep moving from body to body for two or three generations until it finds the right environment that understands its potential and nurtures it, followed by S. Jayachandran Nair's *The Life and Works of Gabriel García Márquez.*

3

Lying in the hotel room in Mexico, Puthoor Higher Secondary School chemistry teacher Mercy Pappachan's one and only Grechayan – Gregory George Mathews – wondered who he was. Was he the Gregory George Mathews who had metamorphosed into Márquez, or was he Márquez who had metamorphosed into Gregory George Mathews, the one who lived in his wife's house in Kundara? It was then that he suddenly saw the amazing similarities between Márquez and himself.

It started with the names – Gabriel García Márquez, Gregory George Mathews. Márquez's wife was called Mercedes Barcha, his wife was called Mercy Pappachan.

Márquez was a journalist; so was he. Márquez's father was a telegraph operator; his father was a telephone operator. Márquez was born in Aracataca; he was born in Kottarakkara. Both of them shared the fish as their star sign. It was after a twelve-year-long affair that Márquez married Mercedes; it was after an affair that lasted eleven years and four months that he married Mercy. Márquez had two boys; he had two girls. Márquez was adept in Spanish, French and Italian; he knew Malayalam, Tamil and Hindi – English was their common regret.

After having discovered a long list of similarities, it was clear that the soul of Márquez, which was probably wandering like a dandelion across the blue skies of Kerala, had no better place to roost than in the body of Gregory George Mathews.

4

'We're leaving. If you want coffee, make some,' Mercy shouted to Gregory, who had not yet gotten out of bed, as she left with the kids on her scooty. It was thanks to the fact that he was a journalist who worked late hours that Mercy allowed him the luxury of sleeping late. Basking in this luxury, Gregory picked up the book that he had been reading the previous day. He now needed to find out how a soul that had come to roost in a new body should be nourished.

He discovered that the best option would be to offer the new soul all the living conditions and experiences that it had enjoyed in its previous body. He also decided that it would be best not to tell another soul about the one that had just possessed his body. Gregory got up from bed with the firm resolve that he would keep everything to himself, brushed his teeth, washed his face, and then got a shock when he glanced at himself in the bathroom mirror. The real Márquez, whom he had seen only in photographs, was smiling at him.

5

After taking the dosa batter out of the fridge, Gregory George Mathews, who used the byline of Gigi Mathews for his columns, called in sick for two days. When he was reminded of the fact that contractual employees are not entitled to medical leave and that it would be considered leave without pay, he muttered, 'As if I care! Go, fling that pittance into the Ithikkara river.' He then washed all the dishes that Mercy Teacher had left in the sink after dinner last night and breakfast this morning. Whether he wrote his column or not, this was one of his non-negotiable chores. After it was all done, he made two dosas and ate them. Mercy Teacher had instructed him to do so only if he was hungry. After that, Gregory – Gigi to his friends – sat down and read *The Life and Works of Gabriel García Márquez* once again. Gregory had decided to befriend Márquez when he started feeling increasingly dejected about the fact that he could not get anywhere with his own novel for five whole years. By then, he had realized that to write a great novel, it was important to read and understand the real-life experiences of great novelists. However, he had never imagined that it would lead to this great a fortune.

Gregory was stunned when he came across more similarities: the fact that both of them desired to have a girl-child; the fact that though he had published his first four books, they had come to nothing; the fact that both of them studied law and then turned to journalism ...

As he read on, Gregory felt that the book was like an autobiography that he would write in the future.

6

That evening, Mercy Teacher came back from school, let herself into the house, flung her bag on the table, and then stumbled upon Gregory, who was sitting on the floor and reading. 'Good God, Grechaya! You did not go to work even today?' she exclaimed loudly. It was a week since he had started binge-reading, after having gone to the city and picked up all the books on Márquez that he could. By now, apart from a table and a chair, he had shifted all the furniture that was in the room to adjacent rooms and had begun to sleep on a thin cotton mat on the floor.

Mercy Teacher persisted. 'You did not go to work today also?'

'Not just today. I might not go to work for many more days,' Gregory replied without lifting his head from the book.

'And pray, why is that? Have you lost this job too?'

'You go get ready. Get the children also ready. Today we are going to the port city of Kochi. We'll spend two weeks there.'

'Have you gone mad, Grechaya? The kids have exams starting Monday, and you want to go on a tour today!' Mercy Teacher went to the kitchen and started on dinner.

'I am running thirty-four. It was at this age that Márquez went on a tour with his family.'

'Who?'

'Márquez – the one and only Gabriel García Márquez. For someone who sees everything as molecules, you will not understand this. That tour was historic – the world still reads about it.' Gregory went to the kitchen, picked up an onion, and peeled it for Mercy in an attempt to win her over.

'Grechaya, do you want chapatis and potato curry for dinner, or do you want me to sit here and listen to your insane story?'

7

Realizing that Mercy Teacher would not relent, Gregory decided to try his luck with the children. He enticed them with all kinds of promises: seeing the port, a ship, a mall, a movie, the metro … Needless to say, the children took up Gregory's cause. Finally, Mercy decided that two weeks wouldn't work, but the weekend after the exams would be fine.

They set off early for Kochi to make the most of two days. But as soon as they had passed Cherthala, Gregory, who was napping in the front seat, suddenly woke up and shouted, 'Got it! I've got that magnificent beginning.' And then he asked the driver to turn back home. Nobody understood the reason, nor did Gregory bother to explain. Mercy tried to tell him that they should spend at least one day in Kochi since the children were really looking forward to the trip and that they had come this far anyway – but Gregory did not yield. 'The line that I was waiting for, for the last twenty years, has come to me like a revelation. We have no option but to go back. A village beside the Ithikkara river. The novel of a family that ruled over the land for five generations spanning a hundred years. The first version will have 1,300 pages. That will be edited down to a beautiful novel which has just 490 pages. I will use forty-eight writing pads for that. And I will smoke 30,000 cigarettes in the process. You need to understand that this aborted journey is part of a magnificent enterprise. You will realize the value of your sacrifice only when history extols this moment tomorrow.'

The trip ended somewhere between Mercy's clenched teeth, the children's tears, and the highly suspicious glances of the driver.

8

'Mercy dear, isn't there the eight cents of land that you inherited from your mother lying unsold somewhere in Kottarakkara?' Mercy was folding the children's clothes. 'What if there is?' she asked without looking up from what she was doing.

'We need to sell that immediately, Mercy.'

'My mother and I will decide whether to sell it or not in time. Grechaya, tell me what your problem is.'

'I am going on a train journey with your mother to Kottarakkara for that.'

'With my mother?'

'I was supposed to go with my mother, Mercy. But unfortunately, she died a while ago. So, for the time being, we'll make do with your mother.'

'Have you really gone mad? You want to travel a distance of fifteen kilometres by train?'

'Yes, I have to go by train. Like how Márquez went to Aracataca with his mother. During this journey, I will not speak to your mother. Then she will ask me – "Why are you not saying anything, my son?" Then I will tell her – "Mother, I am writing a novel!"'

'You go write a novel, stand on your head, do whatever you please. But if you want to travel this distance by train, you will have to take your own mother with you from the Kottarakkara Cathedral Cemetery.'

'Mercy, you will kill the natural flow of my novel.'

'Grechaya, go serve the kids dinner and try and put them to sleep. I need to go to the school early in the morning.'

9

Gregory George Mathews walked through the narrow streets of Kollam, where he worked. He was searching for an old hotel where he could stay. But he just couldn't find the right place. The hotels that he liked were not ancient enough. And in locations that were ancient enough, there were no hotels. Finally, Gregory decided to seek refuge in a tea shop that appeared old enough. There was only an old appappan there, who was enjoying his beedi.

'Chetta, one tea.' Though what he really wanted was lime and soda, Gregory decided to settle for what would be convenient for Appappan.

He threw the beedi out, lit the stove and started washing glasses with hot water.

'Chetta, is there any old hotel that also has a whorehouse on this street?'

Appappan turned and glared at Gregory. Though he was a journalist aspiring to be a novelist, Gregory lacked that brash courage, so he decided that an explanation was warranted in the current context.

'Don't misunderstand me. I am not that type. I just want to write a novel. I need to stay in a hotel that has many sex workers. I will become their close friend. They will wash my clothes for me, I will write letters for them. On rainy nights, they will share their hot soup with me. In return, I will sing songs for them. I will listen to their mutterings and their conversations filled with pain from the other side of the thin wall. And steeped in this surreal world, I will write my novel.'

Appappan kept the glass that he was washing back on the rack. Gregory sensed that something was wrong.

'Chetta, have you heard of Barranquilla?' Appappan switched off the stove on which he had kept the water to boil.

'Chetta, have you heard that Márquez started writing his first novel in a hotel on the notorious crime street in Barranquilla?'

Appappan turned and faced Gregory.

'I will hire a room here. Can you run a whorehouse next to it?'

'Pah! Get up you son of a bitch! Whorehouse indeed!'

Gregory got up.

'Hmm. You might ridicule me now. But one day you will stand in front of me just like Márquez's landlord did to get his autograph.'

10

What Mercy saw when she returned home from school one day really shocked her. The fridge, the television, the microwave oven – everything was gone. Thinking that their home had been burgled, she called Gregory. Though he was busy writing a new column called 'The Giraffe', Gregory answered.

'Grechaya! Thieves have taken everything,' she shrieked.

'What? Are you talking about the handwritten manuscript of my book? God! I did not part with it in spite of being offered a crore for it by people who wanted to make it into a movie!' cried Gregory.

'Who wants your handwritten manuscript? That is lying on the table. I was talking about our fridge and TV.'

'Oh! You scared the living daylights out of me. I sold all that.'

'Sold? Why?'

'To pay back our debt.'

'What do you mean pay back our debt? What debt do you have when the thirty lakhs that my father deposited in the bank is lying there along with all the accumulated interest?'

'Shhh! I am planning to write a prologue that says that while I was creating my dream novel, we went through acute poverty, that we stayed in rented houses with the help of our friends, that we were evicted many times because we could not pay rent, that we had to sleep in railway stations and bus stands ... The critics should read that and be shocked. Mercy dear, you have no idea of the many paths a novelist has to navigate.'

II

It was late when Gregory reached home that night. He had had a couple of drinks with his friends. He had to ring the doorbell and wait outside for quite a while. It was when he was about to ring the doorbell again that the door opened.

Gregory was taken aback by Mercy's attire and expression. The Mercy Teacher who normally wore a churidar or a nightie, was now wearing a pair of pyjamas and a kurta. She had a cowboy hat on her head, and was beaming. Gregory, who was expecting a showdown, felt a bit dizzy.

'What happened to you, Mercy dear? You look totally different.'

'Grechaya! Today, as I was returning from school, a wonderful thing happened. A migratory bird from Peru came and sat on my shoulder, and whispered in my ear, "From today, you will be a writer." Do you know the name of that bird? Llosa.'

'What?!'

'Llosa! Mario Vargas Llosa!'

'Oh! That's a relief. He was a close friend of Márquez. "A total novel" – that is how Llosa described Márquez's *One Hundred Years of Solitude*. I guess, you, too, will write thus about my book, right?'

'Yes, I will. But before that, come close my friend,' Mercy invited Gregory lovingly.

As soon as Gregory came close, Mercy slapped him hard on the face. Unexpected pain seared through Gregory. His eyes watered, blood trickled from his nose. What strength this Peruvian hand has, thought Gregory.

'Now go, sleep in peace Márquez of Kerala. We'll complete the novel tomorrow.'

12

'Mercy dear, tell me, why on earth did you actually hit me?' asked Gregory as they lay in each other's arms that night.

'Grechaya, other than write, you don't really read any books, do you? Forty long years have passed since Llosa hit Márquez. Even today, nobody knows why he did that. So let this, too, remain a secret between us and the world.'

Two Soldiers in Yet Another Arabian Tale

THAT DAY, KOVAL JOHNS AND Edward Henry were on duty at the checkpost on the northern highway of Baghdad. It was afternoon. Traffic was light. A vehicle passed by occasionally, like a camel that had strayed far from the herd.

'No bastard is out today,' Edward muttered, stepping into the makeshift tent on the roadside to escape the overpowering heat.

'Which actually makes things safer for us,' replied Koval, without looking up from the book he was reading, sitting on the sandbag in front of the tent.

'It is this emptiness that is scary. There is no saying when they will all emerge like sphinxes from the desert while you sit and read.'

'Shut up, you fraidy-cat. You have no idea the trouble Jovana took to send this book to me,' Koval said, his anger audible.

There was only one prayer that he had before setting out for the war – that it be over before the new Harry Potter came out. In fact, the day after the war was over, after standing in the queue in front of the control station for a very long time, when it was finally his turn to call home on the satellite phone for a minute, his first question to Jovana was if the next Harry Potter had been released. She promised him that she would send the book as soon as it was, and she kept her promise. God alone knew how difficult it would have been for her to ensure that he got the book. A thousand kisses would not be reward enough after he got back to the States.

Edward left Koval with his Harry Potter and picked up the binoculars again. Even at the far end of the highway that divided the burning desert like a long black river, there was no vehicle in sight. He was relieved that their duty would end in another couple of hours. Edward turned to look at the opposite direction through the powerful binoculars that brought objects many kilometres away into close view. In the distance, he saw the whitewashed wall of a village. As he watched, he saw a group of children walking beside the wall.

'Hey Koval, there are a bunch of kids heading this way just like the other day – keep your gun ready,' said Edward, without taking his eyes off the binoculars.

'Idiot! Take that thing away from your eyes and check if you can even see them,' Koval replied, without looking up from his book.

Edward suddenly realized that he was still looking through the binoculars. He burst out laughing sheepishly. The concern that had filled his mind dissipated.

A few days ago, after completing patrolling duty in a civilian area, when they reached the bus stop, a group of such children had turned up. Edward had gone up to them and said, 'Hi boys!' However, they had looked at him as though he were an alien. And then they spoke to each other in Arabic, said something that sounded like a wisecrack, and laughed. 'We are here to save you,' said one of the guys in the team, in the newly acquired Arabic that they had learned at the camp. The boys burst out laughing as though the guy had cracked a joke. Though everyone took refuge in the fact that the mirth was possibly triggered by the accent, many could not hide their embarrassment. Yet, they started distributing chocolates in an attempt to establish a rapport. But the boys flung the chocolates back at them. And then suddenly, a few boys started pelting stones at them. When Koval took out his gun and screamed, the brats ran away booing. They were not the only ones subject to this treatment – such incidents were increasing.

'Koval, there's a car headed this way,' said Edward, as he continued to look through the binoculars. 'Look, look at the guy in the car – long beard, narrow eyes, turban … This is the guy, have no doubt.'

Koval put the Harry Potter down and stepped out on to the road. Edward handed him the binoculars. 'The boot of the car is open,' said Koval.

'Who knows if there is a bomb in it,' said Edward, with a trace of fear in his voice.

'Don't be so scared, Edward. The law is in our hands.'

'And our lives are in their hands. That bastard will detonate it right here.'

'No! Jovana is waiting for me and my kisses!'

'Shall I fire?'

'Let's find out what he is up to.'

They signalled the approaching vehicle to stop.

The vehicle slowed down and came to a halt near them. Gun in hand, Koval asked the man to step out of the car. The frightened Arab obliged. Edward pushed him with the butt of his gun and shoved him aside. Koval started inspecting the car very thoroughly.

'What's inside the car?' asked Edward.

'Vegetables for the village.'

'Isn't there a bomb hidden under them?'

'No, certainly not. I was there with the people when they were rejoicing as the statue was pulled down. He killed my brothers – all four of them.'

'Aren't you glad that we are here?'

The frightened man nodded in affirmation. And muttered under his breath, 'And your bombs too.'

'What did you say?' asked Edward, as he started frisking the man.

Koval came back after inspecting the car.

'If you see that scoundrel anywhere, please inform us.'

'Hmm.'

'You may go.'

'Ya Allah!' the Arab exclaimed in relief, as he scampered away like a rabbit for dear life.

Koval and Edward smiled at each other with even more relief. It was not surprising considering the fact that for the last many days, all they were hearing of were surprise attacks and the deaths of many a comrade. It had got to a point where there would be sad news awaiting them every day when they got back to the camp after duty. Often, a fellow soldier or a friend would be readied for his final journey back home. As soldiers, they were prepared to die at somebody's hands; but every single day after the war was turning out to be worse than the war itself. The joy of having won the war had worn thin – no, disappeared. What high hopes they had had when they entered Baghdad. Their shot-in-the-arm after winning the war, braving the drifting sand of the blazing desert, was the jubilant welcome the people of Baghdad had given them. But now, every day, the protests, strikes, demonstrations and attacks against the American soldiers, the President, and the army were on the rise. And in the midst of all this were human bombs. Everything else could be managed – but there was no way to spot walking bombs.

'Did you hear what he said? That he was part of the crowd that rejoiced when the statue fell. It is sad that we could not see that happening,' said Koval as he walked back to his Harry Potter.

'When I spoke to her last, Stephana said that she's recorded it for me. Wonder when I will be able to watch that video, lying butt naked on her lap, sipping whisky.'

'I thought that the war would end quickly, and we would be able to go home immediately afterwards. The way things are going, I don't think we'll be back anytime soon.'

'All that, and this bloody heat – wonder how long it will go on like this,' said Edward, sipping from the water bottle hanging outside the tent.

'Definitely for another three months.'

'Good Lord! We'll get fried to death out here by then.' Edward moved as much as possible into the shade that the tent offered.

'I heard that the Indian Army has been invited to come here. If our leaders were smart enough, we could have pushed them into this hellhole and escaped from here.'

'One day we should just step out on to the street and shoot all these mad men. And then sleep peacefully.'

'But that won't solve the problem for good – they keep emerging like flying termites from every corner of the world. Bastards.'

'Why are they so ignorant about the freedom that our country is offering them?'

'Who knows? Their idea of freedom might be quite different from ours.'

Koval ended the conversation using Harry Potter. Edward started gazing at the road through the binoculars. A little later, he saw a man carrying a bag, approaching.

'Koval, there's our man, no doubt. See his big bag? Must be full of explosives.'

A bored Koval put his book aside and walked on to the road. He looked through the binoculars that Edward gave him.

'Yes, he's carrying something heavy.'

'I'll fix the bayonet on your rifle. You should question him. If you have any doubt, give me a signal. I'll see to it that his body is chopped up into pieces smaller than the grains of sand in this desert.'

By then, the man was almost near them. Koval stepped on to the road and pointed his gun at him.

'What's in your bag?'

'It's meat – lamb. I bought it from the next village. It's ages since I had a biryani,' said the man as he kept moving closer towards them. Edward stood with his gun pointed, ready for anything. Koval opened his bag and confirmed that what he had said was true.

'Okay. You can go.'

From simmering in a frying pan of fear, they drowned in an ocean of relief.

Every time someone turned up, mistrust and suspicion flared up in Edward's mind. He is the one who will take my life; he belongs to the Ba'ath Party; he belongs to the Al-Qaeda; he is a religious fanatic; he is a suicide bomber; he is a human bomb…

An old car was speeding towards them from a distance.

'Koval, why is he speeding like that? I'm sure he's one of them.'

Edward stepped on to the road and flagged the car. But the car did not show any sign of slowing down. 'What arrogance – he is not slowing down. He will run us over. Shall I fire before that happens?'

'No. What if he is an innocent guy like the one before?'

'Let God take care of the innocent. We have the right to fire in self-defence.'

'But that should not be based on a hunch.'

'If we wait, he will kill us.'

Edward fired before he finished speaking.

They saw the windshield shatter. The car veered slightly off the road for a few seconds. But it still showed no sign of stopping. Edward ran and hid behind the sandbags like a coward.

'Run, Koval! That's definitely a suicide bomber.'

By then, the car came to an abrupt halt beside Koval. An Arab got out screaming. His face and hands were bleeding from the shattered glass of the windshield.

'Please don't hurt us,' he cried, hands folded. 'My child is really sick, and we are trying to rush him to the hospital.'

Koval leaned forward and looked inside the car. In the back seat, a frail, sick child was lying on the lap of a woman. Feeling sorry, Koval let them go immediately.

Edward, who was watching all this from behind the sandbags, got up and walked towards Koval.

'That was stupid, Koval. Why did you let them go without checking them?'

'He was taking his sick son to the hospital.'

'Who knows if that's just a ruse? They are masters of disguise. What you did was a singular disservice to our government – letting the enemy go giving him the benefit of the doubt. I will have to report this to the command centre.'

'Rogue! You're saying this? I could have shot you dead for running away like a coward.'

'Bastard! You really don't want me to go back home to Stephana, do you? Who knows if you will finish me off in this desert?'

'You deserve to die. The marines don't need cowards.'

'Rogue! This is the second time you are calling me a coward.'

Before he finished speaking, Edward hit Koval with the butt of his rifle. In the midst of that deserted, blazing wilderness, they fought with each other. Koval's forehead sported a gash, Edward lost a tooth.

'Now I doubt if you are also one of them, you bastard – if I let you live…'

Edward pulled out his gun and shot at Koval. He ducked behind the sandbags just in time. Suddenly, a military vehicle appeared on the highway. Both of them jumped up, dusted themselves off, and stood at attention.

'There was the sound of a gunshot as we were approaching. What was that about?' asked the officer who got out of the vehicle.

'This idiot was trying to kill me,' said Koval.

'Yes, I did. If not, this bastard would have killed me.'

The officer put two other soldiers in charge and took Koval and Edward back to the camp. There was bad news awaiting them. Their friend Michael had died in an explosion in the centre of the city. Edward was devastated – he did not go to see Michael's body before it was sent home. He crashed into bed right away, covered himself up with a blanket, and did not even have dinner. Koval, on the other hand, expecting a detailed interrogation, waited dejectedly for a long time in one corner of the camp. But the interrogation did not happen.

Later in the night, when Edward's friends went to persuade him to have dinner, they found that he was running a high fever. Through the night, his friends heard him mumble deliriously as though he were terrified of something, his mumblings interspersed with bouts of crying.

In the morning, the doctor in the camp checked him out and sent him to the United States for further treatment. There, he ended up at the fag end of a long waiting-list of soldiers afflicted with the same symptoms. Behind him, more soldiers, officers, administrators, citizens, why, a whole nation, kept lining up slowly.

The Argentina Jersey

LIKE A STRANGER, I WALKED through the crowded city-street leading to the bus stop. Not in any great hurry, I walked slowly, studying the expressions of people who were walking towards me, going in the other direction. Especially the expressions of young people – people who were my age. How exuberant they seemed. As though in a rush to go conquer something to try and keep pace with racing time. As these avatars of confidence walked past in their creaseless trousers, full-sleeved shirts, ties and shoes, swinging their attaché cases, here I was, clad in a single dhoti and rubber slippers. I suddenly felt very small.

The street-hawker, robbing the pedestrians of their footpath, sat by his various piles of garments, trying to ward off the harsh afternoon sun with a handkerchief, shouting for the entire street to hear, 'Discount sale, discount sale, very low prices for all items!'

Though my pocket was nearly empty, I paused. What if he had something that might fit the measure of my penury?

Right from the day school reopened, the kids had been clamouring for new clothes. Sad that I could not fulfil even the smallest of their wishes, I would affectionately pull them close to me and say, 'Achan will soon get a lot of money, and then I'll buy you everything that you want.'

'When will you get the money, Acha?'

'Tomorrow.'

My answer always was, 'Tomorrow'.

Though the children had given up hope at some point, I had not. Filled with that hope, when I'd go to Mathukuttychayan's shop to find out the sales figures of my Priyanka Soap, he would say, 'My dear Siva, in this day and age, who wants your local soap? Everyone wants soaps the girls bathing on television use. Why don't you release an ad on TV?'

'Do you think that I don't want to? "Breathtaking Fragrance. Total Skin Protection. Priyanka Ayurvedic Soap" – I even have the caption in mind. But all I can do is dream.'

It was the government's self-employment scheme that had inspired me to take a bank loan and start manufacturing Priyanka Soap. It was all okay in the beginning. People used to be curious enough to buy it. But somewhere along the way, they lost interest. Like Mathukuttychayan says, if we force them to buy it, they get irritated: 'Priyanka Soap? We've never seen an ad for this anywhere.' I don't have the money to print a notice, let alone create an advertisement to air on television.

My Priyanka was one of the many indigenous products that were gathering dust in shops without any sale whatsoever. Mathukuttychayan repeated his usual bleat today as well. In spite of that, if he stretched out a hundred-rupee note at the end of it all, it was probably because he sensed how wretched my plight was. That note sat securely in my pocket, the same pocket that also contained the long list of absolute necessities my wife had written down, which were to be bought using the money I would make that day. But none of that would be possible now. Maybe the children can get what they've been wanting for long. I became one of the people standing around a pile of clothes. A few of them asked if the stiches would hold. A few of them voiced the fear that the colour might run. Some bargained ruthlessly. I picked up a couple of pieces and looked at them. They were not bad. I asked what the price was. 'One hundred and twenty-five rupees!' I had two children. So I pretended that I did not quite like the pieces and started searching for something else.

'Take it, brother … it's good-quality stuff. If you go to a big shop, you will have to pay at least four hundred rupees for this,' the vendor said, trying to egg me on.

'I'll take something a bit cheaper.'

'Take the same thing, brother. I'll give it to you at a lesser price.'

'How much less?'

'Give me fifteen less.'

'No, it's okay.' I turned away disappointed. I had two children. And I had only hundred rupees in my pocket.

'Do you have something cheaper than this?' I asked and started rummaging once again hopefully.

'Brother, tell me what your budget is.'

'Let's say fifty rupees…' My voice was feeble.

'Bro, these days it's hard to get a decent underwear for fifty rupees.'

I hung my head in shame. As I was walking away dejected, he called me from behind.

'Wait, brother. I'll give you something that will work for you.'

I walked back expectantly.

He opened a cardboard box kept behind him and took out a handful of T-shirts, all of them with blue and white stripes. I liked them – they looked beautiful; and they would fit the children. T-shirts were anyway the in-thing. So I was convinced that the children would love it.

'These are only fifty a piece?' I asked eagerly.

'It's hundred. But considering the situation you are in, I'll give it to you for fifty.'

I warmed up to him.

At least there was one person in the world who understood my predicament.

I pointed to two T-shirts that I thought would fit the children and he quickly wrapped them up for me.

My eyes exuded gratitude. I gave him the money and walked towards the bus stand.

~

'This looks like the T-shirt that football players wear,' said Meenakshi as soon as she saw them.

'What are you saying? You don't know anything. Our kids too should wear clothes that are modern. If not, people will make fun of them.'

'Whatever you say, I really don't like this. We should have just got two shirts stitched by Narayanettan.'

'That would be typically local – you need to understand that such things are not in fashion any more. You will get to like these in time. They will last long, they're easy to wash, and really easy to wear. From now on, I'm sure our kids will wear these most of the time.'

When the kids, after they came back from school, saw their new clothes, they were happy. They hugged and kissed me. 'It's so nice, Acha,' they said, put on their new T-shirts immediately, and jumped around joyously. They took them off before going to bed only because their mother scolded them. Despite all the problems, seeing them so overjoyed, my eyes welled up.

'Look how happy they are. Only you did not like the T-shirts.'

'The deadline we committed to the bank is tomorrow,' Meenakshi changed the subject.

'I remember. I'll speak to the manager once again and see.'

'How many times have we asked for an extension? Do you think he will agree?'

'If he agrees, he agrees. If not, let them take away everything we have. What else can we do?'

'What wonderful promises the government made – self-sufficiency, subsidy, low interest … But they were all like promises written on water.'

'Now we have no option but to bear the consequences,' I said, echoing her helplessness.

The next day, the children got ready to go to school earlier than usual. In their eagerness to show their friends the new T-shirts their father had bought for them, they ran out with their books, breakfast half-finished, ignoring their mother's admonitions. I left for the bank right after they left for school.

When I returned late that night, tired after a long day, I heard the children crying as I was exchanging pleasantries with my neighbour at the gate. I rushed in. The T-shirts were lying abandoned in the verandah as though they had been flung out. For a moment I stood stupefied, not knowing what had happened to the joy that had filled the house the previous night. As soon as they saw me, the kids ran out. 'Acha, we don't want these T-shirts.'

'Why? What happened?'

They continued to cry without giving me a reply. I asked Meenakshi what the matter was. 'I'd told you yesterday itself that these are worn by football players and won't work.'

'Oh, is that the reason?'

I drew the children close to me. 'So what if they are worn by football players? You should be happy about that.'

'No, Acha. All the kids made fun of us. These T-shirts belong to the losers.'

'Belong to the losers? I don't understand, Meenakshi.'

'Look, this is why I keep telling you that you need to be aware of what is happening in the world. This was the jersey of the Argentina team that lost the World Cup. The street-side vendor dumped the T-shirts on you because he knew they might never get sold. Understand?' Meenakshi walked back into the house in a huff.

'Acha, we don't want the T-shirts of the losers. Just get us the T-shirts of the winners.'

I did not reply. I held them close and walked into the house. I had just been served a notice by the bank that they would be confiscating my house because I was unable to service the loan. Yet, just to calm them down, I said, 'These are the T-shirts that will suit us for now, boys.'

'You wear it Acha, we don't want it,' the elder one said in anger.

I turned to Meenakshi for support.

'What they said is right,' she said, turning away. 'It will suit you. You should wear it.'

I refrained from telling her what I wanted to – that our house would be taken by the bank.

Beaten, I left the house and started to walk.

I got back sometime late in the night.

The T-shirts were still lying in the verandah. It was then that I understood how much Meenakshi and the kids hated them. I sat in the dark verandah for a while. There was no sound from inside. They must have gone to sleep. I was hoping that Meenakshi would stay awake, waiting for me to return. But I did not have the courage to find out if she was up.

I picked up the T-shirts. White and blue stripes, one following the other. The jersey of Argentina, the country that had set out to conquer the world but were totally defeated. The kids were right – this would work only for me. The one who was truly defeated.

I walked to the soap manufacturing unit within our compound. What was once my beacon of hope now seemed like a house of ghosts. I did not feel like switching on the light. The costly equipment that I had bought was gathering dust. The boiling pan, drying chamber, chipping machine, amalgamator, plodder machine, the moulds … Though bought entirely using a bank loan, this was an enterprise worth lakhs that one could use to keep the lender at bay. But from now on, it would not be his. It would belong to the bank. Confiscated goods. I sat tired amid the machinery for a long time. A blanket of emptiness slowly engulfed my consciousness. In that tight, ill-fitting T-shirt, I felt like a clown. And then, with a prayer that my children would one day be able to wear the jerseys of winners, I downed the bottle of Furadan I had bought for my entire family.

A Chapter from My Red Sea Book

THERE IS NO MAN WHO has seen the world like a sailor has. There is no continent, no folklore he does not know. There is no waterway he cannot fathom. He holds the wind and the sea in his heart, both as familiar to him as the lines on the palms of his hands. His experiences and his memories are what the future accepts as history. I know that you expect a great many stories from me, the person whom you honour and respect as the most experienced sailor of the great Roman Empire. In fact, it is this alone that inspired me to overcome the challenges posed by my weather-beaten body and write this travelogue. In the chapters that went before, I filled you in on the customs and ways of life of the people who inhabit every land that I set foot on. In this chapter, I'd like to share with you the most spectacular experience I've ever had from among the hundreds of voyages that I undertook on the Red Sea – a secret I have never shared with anyone in this world.

Our fleet of ships was then anchored at the port of Berenice, about 1800 stadia away from Myos Hormos. Our next destination was the port of Berbera. The ships were being loaded with cargo – it would take another three or four days for all the preparations for the journey to be completed. Until then, since we sailors had nothing in particular to do, we had our fill of wine and Phoenician women in the city. You can well imagine the joie de vivre of a sailor who finally sets foot on land. It was when we were wandering about in the city that he came and met me for the first time. We were at an inn. He was a middle-aged man who did not command any attention. He had streaks of grey in his hair and his beard. A glance was all it took for my seasoned eyes to figure out that he was a Jew. So I gifted him the lack of attention that he deserved. Yet he came right up to me and asked me if I was Cephalus, the First Captain of the fleet of ships sailing to Berbera the next day. I nodded in the affirmative.

'That's a relief,' he said. 'I've been wandering the city for days looking for you. If you would allow me, I would like to travel to Berbera on your ship.'

In every city, there would be people such as this who would request permission to travel, especially to Berenice and Alexandria. Most of them were Jews who had left the conflict-ridden zones of Israel, aspiring to go East, settle down, and live there peacefully. They had thus spread themselves across many countries. Since this was a harmless favour, I had allowed quite a few Jews to cross over in the past. I never charged them a fee; they were only required to help with the routine work on board the ship – furling and unfurling the sail, joining the rowers on the galley and serving food to the crew. In fact, none of these passengers had the means to make even a token payment to travel on our cargo ships. And I never ever asked them the purpose of their journey. For the same reason, I've often sailed into dire straits. At times, it would be those stealthy rebels fighting against Rome who would find their way into the ship. Halfway through the journey, they would try to sink the ship, at times with the help of pirates, to take revenge on Rome. And then a wretched battle would begin. I've had to fling quite a few of them into the sea. In the end, I stopped taking passengers with me. So my first instinct was to reject the man's request. Yet, generously drunk, I said, 'Get ready for the voyage – we might leave the day after tomorrow, in the morning.' He thanked me and excused himself, happy that he had achieved his purpose.

He boarded the ship long before it set sail. The weather was perfect that morning. The sea was calm. The helmsman, the oarsmen and the navigator were delighted. I was sure that if the weather held, we would reach Berbera much earlier than estimated. But the sea is like a woman – you can never predict when her mood will change. The sky that was clear for two days suddenly started turning cloudy and dark, threatening to drown my expectations. The wind gained strength, the sea started getting choppy. Before the workers could cover the cargo, rain came down. The helmsman and the oarsmen struggled to control the ship. It was halfway into the month of Epiphi that monsoon began in Egypt and the shores of the Red Sea. Our plan was to reach Berbera before the onset of the monsoon. But the next six hours heralded the monsoon, proving all our calculations wrong. The volatility of the sky and the sea had even a seasoned sailor like me worried. I ran around giving instructions to the crew. My idea was to dock the ship at the nearest port en route. But with each passing minute, things started to slip out of our hands. Every attempt to row and manoeuvre the sail became challenging. In just three hours, we undid all the progress we had made in an entire day. And in the midst of all this, we lost one ship in our fleet to the weather, along with fifteen sailors. It was clear to me that our lives were under threat and that something had to be done urgently. I tried everything in the book – everything that experience had taught me – but we just could not control the ships. It was when I was standing at the helm wondering what to do next that the man appeared before me.

'It was not at the best of times that you boarded my ship. We now need a miracle to see land again' – it was these very words of disappointment that I uttered, words that even the captain of a sinking ship who was fighting a losing battle would not say.

'May I sail the ship?' he asked. There was an astounding ring of confidence in his voice.

'Are you a sailor?' the seaman in me retorted, reluctant to hand over the ship to a stranger even as hope was rapidly sinking.

'No, I have never been at the helm of a ship. But I have faith. I have seen my guru take charge of the sail and steer his boat.'

'Was your guru a sailor? What's his name? Is he an Arab?' I asked anxiously. There was a reason behind these questions. In those days, the Arabs knew of many sea routes and secrets that we did not know. They never shared these with the rest of the world lest they lose their supremacy as seamen. Suddenly I wondered if I might stumble upon a secret or two.

'No, he is neither a sailor nor an Arab. Yet he had that skill.'

'If he was not a sailor, on which sea did he sail?' I asked in anger.

'The Sea of Galilee.'

'Ha. Galilee? Is that even an ocean? Isn't that just a lake? Are you saying that you can sail a ship on the Red Sea in the midst of this dreadful weather after watching your guru manage a boat on a lake?'

Even in that terrible crisis, my Roman arrogance and seafarer's pride surfaced to slight him.

'True. Galilee is perhaps not a big ocean. The waves are small. But the hurricane that lashes out of the Seleucia Mountains is far more powerful than this. My guru was adept at navigating his boat through such storms.'

He had me there – I knew it to be true. Even I, who had sailed the world, was afraid of the hurricanes that came out of the Seleucia Mountain ranges. In that split second, I decided to let him man the ship. The workers looked on in fear as control was handed over to someone who had no knowledge of the sea and sailing. My crew warned me in low tones that this was a dangerous thing to do.

'We are already in danger,' I said. 'There is no new danger. We need to explore every last thing that can help us survive.'

In life, there are points of crisis when we need to let go and allow others to take over. I believed that it was that willingness to take risks that made me fathom the myriad mysteries of the oceans. To the seamen of tomorrow, let me state here and now, that only a brave sailor willing to take risks and experiment will be able to find new sea routes and discover new lands. But then, there are unfortunate times when whatever one does turns out to be a colossal mistake. Fortunately, this was not one of those times. By furling and unfurling the sails and giving instructions to the oarsmen, he took charge of the ship in no time. None of us had ever seen anyone handle the sails in that manner, with that strange timing. I just stood there watching him bring the ship under control in just a few minutes, even as the storm continued to howl and churn the sea. Soon the ship was no longer a plaything in the hands of the wind. The helmsman and the oarsmen who were struggling until then heaved a sigh of relief. And in a short while, the wind that had imperilled the ship became a companion, filling her sails, taking us forward on course. I could not contain my joy. It was not just an escape from the jaws of death, it was also a new discovery that would forever change my life at sea. I hugged, and why, even kissed him – the first time I ever kissed a Jew.

So let me say it loud and clear, here and now – the discovery that the world thinks is mine, in reality, is not mine. It was he who discovered how to tame the monsoon winds and navigate the great seas to reach distant lands. To be more accurate, it was his guru, someone I never knew. My only contribution was that I refined his crude method and made it far more effective. In all my twenty-four years of sailing, I had never seen someone furl the sails obliquely in the direction of the wind and then unfurl them when the wind changes direction, while ensuring that the oarsmen threw their oars in tandem, obliquely and then in reverse. No one had thought of doing this before. All the discoveries of mankind are quite simple – it is just that until they take birth in a sharp-witted mind, they remain problems unsolved.

This discovery changed the very course and history of navigation. It halved the work of the oarsmen, the helmsmen and the navigator. Not only that, but this discovery also helped me cut across the ocean effortlessly and go directly from the shores of the Red Sea to prime ports that were the centres of trade and commerce, like Muziris and Nelcynda. This helped me discover sea routes that the Arabs and the Phoenicians had kept a closely guarded secret until then. This meant that we could now travel to any country in the east fearlessly, by avoiding the pirate-infested waters of Arabia and Persia.

That gave a big fillip to our trade. More than all this, it was because of this one man that I had the fortune to have my name and my life become part of history, without being just one of the thousands of ordinary sailors of this land who would forever remain anonymous.

On that day, in spite of the terrible weather, we reached Berbera safely and on time. Before he left the port, I asked him about his guru. But he left without giving me a clear answer.

Four or five years went by. And then one day, very unexpectedly, I met him at the port of Alvarez. Overjoyed, I took him to the inn that I was staying at and treated him to wine and food. He said that he had completed his mission in Alexandria, Berbera and Alvarez, and was planning to head east. When I asked him what his mission was, he just said that it was one with which his guru had entrusted him. Unfortunately, that was not the time our ships were heading east. In those days, it was difficult to find ships sailing to the east from Alvarez. There were a few ships in that port that were sailing to Opone via Mundus, Mosyllum, Tocina and Rhata ports. There would always be a number of ships sailing to Ocelis from there. Ocelis was a major port where sailors berthed to unload cargo for other ships that catered to countries in the east. I told him that he would be able to reach the eastern countries if he took this route. 'Sure, that's fine with me,' he said, and I saw him off in a ship that belonged to a friend of mine.

After this, I bumped into him at the port of Socotra, exactly two years later. I thought he had returned after visiting the eastern provinces like Chera and Pandya. But he said that on that trip, all he could do was visit the countries enroute to the east. It was then that I realized that he was, after all, not a refugee from Israel, trying to relocate elsewhere. He did not seem to have an ultimate destination and he did not appear too concerned about time or timetables. It seemed like he had something specific to do in every country. He was either a merchant trading with different people in different ports, or a mad traveller, drifting from one exotic land to the other.

I told him that our next destination was the port of Muziris in the east. He was very happy to hear that, and said that it was one place to which he had always wanted to go. So he ended up being with us during that long journey. I say it was a long journey because instead of cutting across the Arabian Sea and heading straight to Muziris, we first visited several ports in the east to pick up cargo. After crossing the Persian Gulf and the Bay of Gedrosia, we reached Barbarcum, the most important of the seven ports of Sindhu, where the Scythia lived. From there we travelled to Barygaza. The journey through the treacherous swamps here was really strenuous. Even the most experienced sailors could have accidents here. It was around this time that the sailors of that region started accompanying and guiding ships to prevent mishaps. We then went on to the ports of Kalyan and Sopara, which fell under the rule of Kushan, purchased goods, and then went on to Muziris.

It was during that long journey that I got to know him better and he started opening up. He was indeed a Jew like I had guessed. He travelled to spread the message of his guru (he had mentioned the name of his guru, but my ageing memory refuses to bring it up; I should have written this piece about ten years ago) from one country to another – especially countries to which Jews had fled in large numbers from Israel. He told me many stories of the marvels that his guru had performed, including the one of how the guru rescued the boat they were all travelling in from the onslaught of a sudden and frightening sea storm by manoeuvring the sails.

Muziris in the Chera kingdom is one place where a large number of Jews lived peacefully then and even now. And that was the reason why he had always wanted to go there.

He disembarked at Muziris. It was almost nine years since we had first sailed together. I since travelled to Muziris and Nelcynda many times to buy pepper and other esoteric and expensive spices. He never returned with us even once. I learned a lot about him from the workers in the port – that he was spreading the word of his guru extensively and that he had set up churches in many countries. Later, when I was there, I came to know that he had died at the hands of the tribals in a forest east of the Chera kingdom.

My reminiscences of this man should ideally end here. But recently, a book titled *Periplus of the Erythraean Sea* surfaced in a very famous library in Rome. What was strange was that the author's name was not mentioned. I was asked if I had authored this detailed and authoritative book – probably because there was nobody in Rome who had travelled as extensively as I had. I said emphatically that I had not authored the book. Then who could it be? I managed to get a copy of the book and read it. All the sea routes and countries mentioned in it were real and authentic. There was nothing that was unreal or imaginary there. The accuracy of information revealed that the author was definitely someone who had travelled the world extensively. Who could the writer be? As I went through the book repeatedly, I could think of only one person who could have authored it – the Jew who was killed in the Chera kingdom thirty years ago. All the voyages in the book matched perfectly with the voyages undertaken by him. But according to the book, the author crossed over from the Chera to the Chola kingdom and then via the Gangamugham, visited China, before getting back to Rome.

What I was puzzled about was this: if it was indeed a Roman who wrote it, why did he choose to hide himself? If he had revealed his name, wouldn't his land and his King have honoured and rewarded him amply? I don't think that there is any fool in Rome who would reject all that and stay anonymous. And if it was the Jew who had written it, why did he spread false word that he had been killed in the jungle? Why did he not travel back with us? Why did he choose to take another road to Rome? Who was his guru? What was the secret agenda that carried him from country to country?

It is not a sailor's job to find answers to these questions. I leave that to the historians and the secret service agents of the King. All I can say is that a secret lies hidden between him and Rome.

Postscript

Did you know that it was in AD 45 that the Roman sailor Hippalus discovered that he could use sails to navigate his way to the countries in the east, including India, using the monsoon winds? It was around the same time that the first ever travelogue, *Periplus of the Erythraean Sea*, that features Kerala in detail, was published. The author of this book is unknown. And yes, it is believed that St. Thomas reached India in AD 54.

Nedumbassery

It was just this morning that Lissy had advised Kunjumon, 'Let others do what they want, let them grow any which way they want. But Chachan, *you* should not get into this.' However, after thinking about it for one whole day, Kunjumon found no reason to accept her advice. So much for all the advice Appan and Lissy had been ladling out all these years. All the people who had started out as drivers along with him were kind of settled by now. Monachan had built a beautiful house, Josekutty had bought a Toyota Innova for himself, Prathapan's children were studying in an English-medium school. He, on the other hand, was still a driver on hire. Enough was enough. Even he needed to achieve a few things. So, pushing Lissy's list of obstacles away, Kunjumon called them in the night and requested that they reserve the following day for him. It was not that he really wanted to, but the pain of pressing needs and the lure of unfulfilled desires suddenly had a vice-like grip on him.

Kunjumon had been waiting for a while for his turn to come. But on that day, contrary to his expectations, he did not get any ride. Some days were like that. There was not a single tourist in sight. And the locals who came out didn't need a taxi either. There was nothing to do other than kill time drinking tea, smoking cigarettes, and making small talk. Kunjumon felt disappointed and angry. But there was no option but to sit and wait. Miss one turn, and the next opportunity would come only after two hundred turns, and that would take at least three days. And what did that mean? One could not accommodate anyone from outside the regular queue even if it were for a short emergency trip. And on days like this, there would be nothing – neither this nor that. All that would be left to do was to go back home empty-handed.

That day, when the last flight landed, Kunjumon was still fifth in the list. He was sure that there wouldn't be enough takers for taxis on that flight and that he might have to wait until the next day for his turn. But as luck would have it, five passengers from that flight queued up in front of the prepaid taxi counter. And then, finally, when his turn was announced, a sudden, hitherto unknown fear crept into his mind.

A little later, when the fifth traveller emerged with the bill for the prepaid taxi in his hand, Kunjumon was standing behind a pillar, calling them on his mobile.

'So, did you get anything?'

'Hmm, I just got a ride,' Kunjumon replied, his voice quivering.

'We've been waiting since morning. Is it a tourist or a local?'

'Local.'

'Then let it go. He won't have anything. We'll try next time.'

'Looks like a rich guy. Not only that, I can't wait any more. I'm desperate.'

'Hmm. Is it a family?'

'No. There's only this man and a kid.'

'Does he have a lot of luggage?'

'Those who come with a lot of baggage don't have any money on them. That I know. It's the guys with minimum luggage who are loaded.'

'We know that. Where's the trip to?'

'From the counter I heard that it was Chengannur.'

'Which route are you taking?'

'Which route will work for you?'

'We're fine with any route you take. Just call when you reach Aluva. We'll decide then. Choose a route that is congested – that way, it will be late enough when you reach here.'

'My hands are trembling,' Kunjumon said.

'That's okay. It's your first time. You will be fine once you have a bit of experience.'

Kunjumon put the phone in his pocket and rushed towards the traveller. He respectfully took his bag and kept it in the boot. He felt a bit disappointed when he sensed that the bag was not very heavy.

The traveller and the child got into the car. Kunjumon closed the door for him and got into the driver's seat. After touching the steering, he made the sign of the cross, touched Mother Mary's picture, kissed it, and then started driving out of the airport. When he reached the main road, he played a song, quite loudly. It was almost as though he wanted to drown the sound of his rapidly increasing heartbeat.

'Could you turn down the volume please?' the traveller asked from behind.

Kunjumon lowered the volume.

'What's your name?' the traveller asked.

Kunjumon detested people who made irrelevant small-talk. Though he felt that there was no need for such pleasantries when you got into a taxi to just go from one place to another, Kunjumon revealed his name to the traveller.

'Where do you stay?'

'Here we go again,' Kunjumon muttered to himself. 'Nearby.'

'Our airlines – they're terrible. The flight was delayed by three hours,' complained the traveller.

'That was quite convenient for us, actually,' Kunjumon muttered to himself again, this time a tad louder. But the traveller did not really latch on.

'What did you say?' he asked, leaning forward.

'I was just saying that it's a regular thing now – flights being late.'

'Yes. I think our train services are better than this ... When do you think we will reach?'

'The traffic is heavy – we need to travel around 150 kilometres. And you know the condition of the road. However fast we go, it will be past ten by the time we get there.'

'It is easier for us to land in Thiruvananthapuram,' the traveller said, leaning forward a bit so that Kunjumon could hear clearly. 'But of late, we land only here, in Kochi. The airport is clean, porters don't harass you, taxi guys don't crowd around you, and I have always felt that the people here are good. Landing in Thiruvananthapuram is like walking into a gangster's den.'

That hit where it hurt for Kunjumon.

He was hearing a compliment about his land and its people from a traveller for the first time – that, too, from a local. Most people end up complaining, connecting all the problems of Kochi and Ernakulam to the Nedumbassery airport.

'Anyway, we are late. Let's stop somewhere and have a cup of tea.'

'If you want to go to a premium restaurant, we'll have to get into the city – which means we'll get stuck in more traffic and be delayed further,' Kunjumon objected.

'No. A small hotel will do. My daughter needs to use the washroom.'

'Then we might as well stop here,' Kunjumon said, pulling up near a small hotel that he knew well.

The traveller and his daughter got out. Kunjumon did not budge from the driver's seat.

'Come, have a cup of tea with us. You have a long drive ahead, don't you?' the traveller invited Kunjumon.

'No, it's okay. Go on, have your tea and come.'

'Have a cup of tea, come,' the traveller insisted.

'No, I really don't want anything now. I don't like tea all that much anyway,' Kunjumon lied.

As the traveller and his daughter entered the hotel, a thought struck Kunjumon. The traveller's bag was in the boot. What if I just take off before he comes out? It was for the first time in ten years that such a thought had occurred to him. But he banished the thought from his mind. That would be a terrible mistake. The traveller has my vehicle number. All my details are there with the airport authorities. However far I manage to go, I'd be caught in less than twenty-four hours. Without 'their' help, it would be impossible for me to pull anything off. The school was asking for ten thousand rupees as donation for Ronnie's admission next week. Where on earth would the money come from? Kunjumon called them on his mobile.

'Where are you?' they asked.

'In Aluva.'

'Are they with you?'

'No. They've gone in to have tea. I was also invited, but I refused. Truth be told, this is the first time a traveller invited me along to have tea.'

'Now, don't get emotional. Tell us which route you are going to take.'

'I'm thinking of taking the highway.'

'No. There could be police around. You do one thing – take the Vaikom–Ettumanoor road and go via Kottayam.'

'That will be better, right?'

'There are plenty of stretches where there will be no people or houses. We'll be able to pull it off without too much trouble. Call if you have to. If not, we'll go ahead as planned.'

By then the traveller and his daughter returned. Kunjumon started the car, and they continued the journey.

'Though small, the restaurant was very clean. Unlike a few places where you won't even want to pee.' The traveller started talking again. Kunjumon did not respond to that. He thought that his disinterest would dissuade the traveller, but the latter was not the kind who would give up so easily.

'Have you been doing this for long?'

'Yes, it's been quite a while. I got this job in exchange for giving up my land for the airport.'

'Is this your own car?'

'No, this is on rent.'

'Even after all these years? You should have got your own vehicle by now,' the traveller said, almost accusingly.

'All that will never happen,' said Kunjumon, half in disappointment and half in anger.

'It will happen if you set your mind to it,' the traveller encouraged Kunjumon.

'Yes, it would have happened if I had really wanted it to. I let things slide until now. But from today, I've decided that I will make an attempt. Yes, from today...'

It was very clear that the traveller did not comprehend the real meaning of Kunjumon's words. Which was probably why he changed the subject.

'There's no need to go so fast. Driving on these roads always scares me,' the traveller said, touching Kunjumon's shoulder with his hand to emphasize what he had just said. 'In all these years, have you ever had an accident?'

'Luckily, no,' Kunjumon said, thinking of Lissy, Ammu and Ronnie, and the prayers of his Appachan and Ammachi.

'My father always used to say that if you are good at heart, no road will ever let you down,' said the traveller. 'My father was also a driver.'

'In the State Transport Department?'

'No. He was a taxi driver like you. It was the first taxi in our village. He drove for thirty years, and he never even scratched the vehicle once.'

Suddenly Kunjumon's mobile started singing 'The Lord of Israel'.

Kunjumon answered. They were calling.

'Where have you reached?'

'Just crossed Kalamassery.'

'Hmm. Rameshan will wait at Thrippunithura.'

'There's heavy traffic. We might get there later than expected.'

'That's okay. We'll call.'

They cut the call.

'That was from home – they wanted to know when I'd get back,' Kunjumon explained on his own, just so that the traveller did not feel suspicious.

'Yes, people at home will always be anxious until you get back. Especially if you are driving in the night. You have no idea how many sleepless nights I've spent waiting to hear the sound of my father's car come back home … There were no mobiles then. There was no way of knowing anything until the person physically came back home. My mother, too, would not sleep until he got back. There's no describing the wave of relief that sweeps over you when you see the headlights stream in through the window as he drives in during some part of the night. I don't think you'll quite understand that feeling, Kunjumon. Only your children will.'

Kunjumon thought of his son Ronnie who would hug his mother and keep asking her when his father would come home. And then he thought of his daughter Ammu who would always insist on sleeping next to her father. These thoughts disturbed him. Worried that they might drain his courage, he tried to think about how Rameshan would be waiting for him at Thrippunithura. And then thought of the ten thousand rupees that had to be given to the school to secure Ronnie's admission.

Suddenly, it started drizzling. The wind blew the rain sideways. When Kunjumon started rolling up the windows, the traveller dissuaded him.

'Let me feel the cool breeze. It's such a long time since I saw rain.'

The traveller's daughter stuck her hand out in an attempt to catch the rain.

'Please don't do that. There are vehicles passing by, it's dangerous,' said Kunjumon, his voice filled with genuine concern.

Kunjumon thought of Ronnie again. Thought of his desire to educate him so that he would become successful. Thought of the reality that it would not be possible with the meagre income of a taxi driver. Thought of the get-rich-quick plan that helped Monachan build a house, Josekutty buy a Toyota Innova and Prathapan educate his children in an English-medium school.

The little girl was lulled to sleep by the cool breeze. Dusk was rapidly giving way to night. The streetlamps lit up. It started raining heavily. There was no option but to roll up the windows. The drain overflowed on to the road. The vehicles started moving slowly. At times, they moved at a snail's pace; at times, they had to sit still and wait endlessly for the traffic to start moving again.

'Sir, where do you work?' Kunjumon had a sudden urge to know more about the traveller.

The traveller told him the name of the city in which he worked.

'Is it a really great job?'

'It's not all that much of a great job, but it does give me the money to live really well.'

'Did your father have his own taxi?'

'In the beginning, he was just a driver on hire. But much later, he took a loan and bought a car. I still remember going to Pondicherry with my father and a car mechanic from a nearby workshop to buy the car. It was a black Ambassador. It was as though we had bought a piece of paradise…'

'Will anyone be able to buy a car from the money earned by working as a driver for hire? Be able to educate his children well? He must have had some business on the side. Was it chit funds?' Kunjumon wondered aloud, half to himself, half to the traveller.

'No, nothing of the sort. He taught us – demonstrated, in fact – that if we learn to live based on our resources, a driver who does not have his own car can very well make ends meet. He built his own house, bought his own car, educated me well in the city, got my two sisters married – all from that small income of his.'

By then, they had reached Thrippunithura. It was still raining. Suddenly, someone stepped on to the road and flagged their car. But Kunjumon kept driving as though he had not seen anything.

The traveller, though, had seen the man.

'Oh, someone wanted us to stop.'

'Must be someone who was waiting for a bus … It's okay,' Kunjumon said dismissively.

'Must have been someone who was waiting endlessly. We should have stopped.'

'Sir, you're not scared to do that?' Kunjumon asked in astonishment.

'Scared? About what?'

'To allow strangers to get into the car? Most people would not do that. Which is why I asked.'

Kunjumon's heart was aflutter when he said that. A short while later, his mobile began to sing again.

'Hello.'

'Bastard! Why on earth did you not stop when we flagged your car?'

'I did not see anything in this rain.'

'Did not see? I had told you clearly where we would be.'

'I told you, I did not see you.'

'It's okay. Drive slowly. We're behind you. We have to do this before you reach Vaikom.'

Though Kunjumon agreed before hanging up, he stepped on the accelerator.

'I have travelled through many unknown cities during the day as well as night, Kunjumon – Mumbai, Allahabad, Imphal, Bilaspur, Bhubaneswar, Jammu, Trichy … That, too, in taxis that belong to people from different parts of India. Nobody has put my life in any danger thus far. Then why on earth should I be afraid in my own home state? I've never felt that Kerala is the terrible place that the media make it out to be and people from other states perceive it to be. Most people here have a lot of goodness in them. And as far as you go, one look and I knew I could trust you. I have absolutely no fear of travelling in this car.'

Kunjumon's heart fluttered again.

'But I'm afraid I never give lifts to strangers. One cannot fathom what kind of people they are,' replied Kunjumon.

'Very true. One night my father went on a trip like this. Two youngsters came in the evening and hired his car. One guy sat in the font and the other sat in the back. They wandered around until after midnight. When they were in a dark bylane, the guy who was sitting in the back suddenly put a towel around my father's neck and held him firmly to the seat. The guy sitting in the front took a knife and stabbed my father in the chest.'

The car was going through a dark patch. None of the streetlights there were working. All of a sudden, a bike raced forward from behind and blocked the path of Kunjumon's car. For a split second, Kunjumon was flustered. He then swerved and avoided him, averting an accident. 'Careful, careful!' cried the traveller. 'These bikers are the limit – there's no end to the accidents that happen every day thanks to their carelessness. But they'll never learn.'

'Tell me what happened to your father.' The anxiety in Kunjumon's voice surprised the traveller.

'In spite of almost being strangled and stabbed, my father did not give up. He used all his strength to fight them after stopping the car without losing control. He kicked out the guy sitting in the front, grabbed the hair of the man behind him and managed to free himself from his vice-like grip before turning around and hitting him hard.'

The bike was still following Kunjumon's car. So was another car, which kept dimming its lights constantly in an attempt to overtake Kunjumon. But Kunjumon drove through the middle of the road as fast as he could without allowing them to overtake him. Kunjumon's mobile sang once again, but he did not respond.

'The people in the vicinity came rushing, hearing the commotion and caught hold of the two youngsters and saved my father. This job can be quite dangerous, right?'

In that rain, Kunjumon broke out into a sweat, not knowing how to respond.

'You said they stabbed him in the chest…?'

'It was not deep, just a superficial wound. But he still has that mark on his chest. Even today, he keeps running his hand over it and saying that if you have goodness in you, your road and your vehicle will never let you down.'

'Your father taught you a lot, did he not?' Kunjumon asked the traveller as though he did not quite believe everything that he had said until now.

'Yes. And he was willing to teach me more. But I left in search of a job.'

'Your father built his own house, did he not?'

'Yes, a small house, which was all we needed to live in.'

'Your father got your two sisters married, did he not?'

'Yes. Both of them got married before I got a job.'

'Did he do all this with the money he made as a driver?'

'I told you, yes.'

Kunjumon's questions made it amply clear that he was caught in a whirlwind of disbelief, which was disconcerting for the traveller, who suddenly started feeling that Kunjumon was a stranger. But Kunjumon persisted with his questions.

'Sir, your father did not have any side-business, right?'

'No, Kunjumon. He would never even take things left behind accidentally by travellers. Once he travelled ten kilometres to return an umbrella someone had left behind. Why, he even returned a purse full of money that he found in the car!'

'A driver will be able to raise his children well with just the money he makes, right sir?' Kunjumon asked again, as though he still had a doubt.

'Yes, Kunjumon. It's possible. The person sitting in your backseat is proof enough.'

With each question, the speed of the car kept increasing. Though the traveller kept asking him to slow down, Kunjumon did not even hear him. All he wanted to do was travel as fast as possible to escape from their clutches.

'Don't go so fast, I'm starting to get scared. We might have an accident,' the traveller chided him from behind.

'If you have goodness in your heart, your road and your vehicle will never let you down,' Kunjumon said.

The traveller did not see Kunjumon run his hand over his chest to make sure that the mark of the wound was still there.

The Enemy

I WAS DESPERATE TO REACH my destination. I walked fast, really fast. In fact, I was somewhere between walking and running. I was still piqued about the time I had wasted waiting for the bus. I kept hoping that I would get a ride. But the roads were already alarmingly empty. The few people I met on the road warned me that they could appear any minute. But my mission was very important – there was no way I could turn around and go back.

And then, suddenly, I saw them in the distance. They were moving towards me from afar, like a giant river that had finally broken the dam which had contained it for ages. The aggression in their voices hit me even from this distance. For a moment, I stood shocked. Then I summoned up all my courage and started walking as far inward from the kerb as possible. After all, I'm just a passerby, I am not their enemy; not their friend either, perhaps.

As they inched closer, my fear grew. But I kept moving forward. And then, when the first wave of people reached me, I moved out of their way as much as possible. If I had

had a place to hide, I would have – like all the people who were hiding behind the closed doors of their homes and the downed shutters of their shops. I could not locate any place where I, too, could hide. So I tried to be as obscure as possible, as insignificant an obstacle as possible.

The fiery eyes of one group of people fell on me. My heart skipped a beat. But I clung on to the last vestiges of courage I had and continued to stand still on the pavement. They kept passing me by. Many of them laid their eyes on me. It seemed as though they were shouting slogans at me, brandishing bloodstained weapons in their hands. They kept flowing endlessly, throwing aggressive threats and warnings into the air.

No, I am not their enemy; not their friend either, perhaps. I suddenly realized that this was the reason why they were furious; this was why more and more eyes fell on my solitary figure.

Fear – uncontrollable fear – began to swallow me like a python. The aggression directed at me kept getting louder. Now I knew it clearly – I was one of their targets. Some of them scraped my clothes with their weapons. More weapons were moving in my direction.

And then, for a split second, I thought about my family who would be waiting anxiously for me to return. In no time, I was one with the gang, walking with them, shouting slogans louder than the others. Somebody thrust a weapon into my hand. I began flaunting it at other helpless passersby.

Solapur

THEY LOCKED THE HOUSE AND left at six in the morning. They'd be able to catch the first bus to Solapur if they reached the main road by seven. They had to reach Pune by afternoon at the very least. In fact, that is what Gopal had instructed them to do. To be safe, Shobhi had packed a few chapatis and vegetable curry. She had woken up at four in the morning to make them. Shobhi was destined to be constantly rebuked by Chandammai, who kept saying that she was the kind of girl who would not wake up if the sun, making its way across her face, shone even on her ass. She refused to understand Shobhi's ailments and her medications. 'Lazy bitch,' she would always say, grimacing.

'You've taken the mobile, haven't you?' Though Shobhi had asked this question a couple of times already, as she crossed the barren rivulet in the middle of the paddy field, she wanted Hanumanta to reassure her once again. He patted his pocket and replied in the affirmative once again.

'Be careful. The bus will be full of pickpockets from Barshi. You know how much that thing costs,' Shobhi said.

'Yes, I do. I'll take care of it. I won't fall asleep,' Hanumanta said, clutching his pocket.

They had to wait a while below the tree on which bats practised yoga in their sleep. By then people had started gathering at Ram Bapu's dhaba for their morning black tea. Though they were hoping that there would be nobody who'd know them, Lakhu Bappa, the wandering fortune-teller, whose parrot picked cards for him, had already recognized them.

'Where are the two of you off to in the morning?' he asked loudly.

'Solapur. To pick up some fabric.' That was the first lie that came to Hanumanta's mind.

'To buy clothing material? That, too, in these terrible times? Did you win a lottery or something? Or did someone loan you black money?'

Thankfully, Hanumanta did not have to reply. The bus arrived raising a cloud of dust and stopped right in between them, hiding one from the other.

There were only a few people in the bus. Both of them found seats. Hanumanta sat looking at the fog of dust outside. It lay like a cover of fear over the parched fields, which were once full of wheat and lentils. These were fields where Hanumanta and Shobhi had worked for years on end, fields which had gifted them happiness. But the drought had laid the fields and their lives barren. Hanumanta sighed.

'You'll catch a cold. Wrap yourself up well.' Shobhi gave her shawl to Hanumanta.

'No. I'll cover my ears.' Hanumanta dragged down the pheta on his head over his ears.

As the bus gathered speed and the breeze picked up, Hanumanta clutched the mobile phone in his pocket and held it close to his chest, as though it were a scrap of paper that might fly away. 'That is switched off, right?' Shobhi wanted to reconfirm. 'Don't drain the power. They don't have electricity in their house. Nor do their neighbours. To charge their mobile phones, they have to go to Prahladan's barber shop near the village market, which is quite far away. And he charges ten rupees for that.' This was the phone that Gopal had given them the last time he'd paid them a visit.

'You can pay me in instalments. We will move closer to digital India only when ordinary folks like you start using new-age technology,' Gopal had said, handing over the mobile phone to Hanumanta.

'But Gopal ji, I don't know how to take pictures and all on this,' Hanumanta said a bit helplessly.

'Hanumanta! You know how to ride a bicycle, drive a tractor, operate the water pump and the thresher – a mobile phone is nothing. I'll make you an ace in two hours, wait and see!'

He was right. Hanumanta learned all the shortcuts much faster than expected. It was the same mobile that lay switched off, like a fledgling that could not fly, in Hanumanta's pocket.

They had to wait for a long time in Solapur to get a bus. Most of the buses that were going to Pune were plush air-conditioned buses which they could not afford. When he heard the fare, he felt that he should have travelled alone. But then, that would not have worked. Patil wanted to meet both of them. 'It's okay. When we go back, instead of this mobile, we will have a pocketful of cash. Then we can sit back in the cool comfort of an AC bus,' Shobhi comforted Hanumanta. Finally, they got a regular bus – one that literally crawled along, one that stopped everywhere.

'Wonder if Jani has eaten anything. If not, that mother of yours would have chewed her head off by now.' Shobhi worried, sitting in the bus.

'Aai is angry only with you. She is fond of her.' Hanumanta held Shobhi's hand and comforted her. Shobhi was really not in favour of leaving her daughter with Chandammai. But they did not have an option. Without knowing if they would be able to come back the same day, and even if they did, not knowing how late they might be, Hanumanta was forced to leave Jani with his mother, who lived four streets away.

Chandammai's quarrel started the day he married Shobhi, who was the daughter of the sweeper-woman in the market of Chapalgaon, where Hanumanta went to buy seeds and sell produce. Shobhi used to come along with her mother to clean the marketplace. It was there that Hanumanta saw her for the first time and came to like her. 'That bitch who sweeps the market is way lower to us in caste' – this was Chandammai's problem. Those days, Hanumanta used to ask her, 'Why "we" and "them"? Who's lower than us in this world, Aai?' And she, furious, would reply, 'You – without as much as a speck of potato dust in your head – there are fifteen different sects in our own caste. And they are the lowest in the rung.' In spite of Chandammai weeping over the fact that they would lose face if he married her, Hanumanta did not relent. He went ahead and married Shobhi. In spite of them having moved out, in spite of a granddaughter, in spite of many years having gone by, Hanumanta's mother Chandammai's dissent persisted. It was with her that they had entrusted Jani, and that was why Shobhi was anxious.

'Why are you leaving your daughter with her grandmother, Hanumanta? Are you guys planning to commit suicide or something?' Bhimshah, the rock-cutter who was playing with his kids on the side of the road, had asked him that morning.

'Not immediately, Bhimshah. Will let you know when the time comes,' said Hanumanta. Shobhi quipped, 'Don't forget to bring the TV channels along.'

'If the weather continues like this, that time will come quickly for everyone,' Bhimshah had muttered to himself.

They were unable to reach Pune on time as planned. Hanumanta switched on the mobile when they reached the Pune bus stop and called Gopal. He yelled at them: 'Are you saying that Patil Sahib has to wait for a whole day for two bandicoots to turn up? No wonder Chandammai says that you are the kind who sleep until the sun burns your asses. This is why you people never get anywhere in life…' Gopal kept pouring his anger out. Hanumanta listened quietly. Gopal hung up saying he would come over to the bus stop.

Gopal soon reached the bus stand in an auto, picked them up and took them to Patil's shop. Patil was a young man under thirty. But he had the arrogance of forty, the cunning of fifty, and the maturity of sixty. 'Patil Sahib, these are the people I spoke to you about,' Gopal introduced them.

'Wait upstairs. I'll come and take a look,' Patil said very gravely and sent them up to the terrace above the shop.

They were really hungry by then. Shobhi opened the packet in her bag. They sat on the terrace and shared the chapatis and the vegetable curry that had started to go bad.

'Let me take a look,' said Gopal, stretching out his hand for the mobile after placing water in front of them.

'No, Gopal ji. We are embarrassed.' Hanumanta clutched his pocket again. 'No brother, it will be a shame if someone in our village sees it. That is why we travelled all the way to Pune. If not, we could have sold it in Solapur itself.' Shobhi nodded in agreement. Though her stupidity amused Gopal, he did not allow it to register on his face. 'Why should you be embarrassed in front of me, Hanumanta? After Patil Sahib sees it, if you want me to put in a word as to how good it is and get you some more money, shouldn't I, too, have seen it?' Hanumanta's grip on his pocket eased. Very reluctantly, he gave the mobile to Gopal. Shobhi lowered her face and looked at the remaining chapatis.

It happened one evening three months ago. Hanumanta was smoking in Ram Bapu's dhaba. Gopal arrived, sat next to him, took his mobile out, and showed him a few pictures secretly.

Gopal was the son of Chandu Lal, who was the only policeman in that village; he was also the most educated guy there. He had many big businesses in Pune. He always wore the smell of tobacco on him. He came to the village once in a while, would stay in his house for a few days and then return. It was one of those days.

Hanumanta was shocked to see the pictures. Though he had heard that such pictures were available, he himself had never seen one. Gopal then showed him a few videos on the mobile. 'From where do you get all this, Gopal ji?' Hanumanta asked, his mouth open, partly in fear.

'These are easily available on the internet. But the attraction to these kinds of white-skinned women is now waning. The demand now is for ordinary villagers like us. There's a lot of money in it. For one photograph, you'll get as much money as you would have got for working in the fields for one year. I am here to help people who want to make money. You need to be willing, of course,' Gopal muttered, as though to himself.

Hanumanta finished his tea and left without replying, as though he had not heard anything.

That night, Hanumanta hardly slept. Shobhi thought that it was because they had fought that evening over the fact that there wasn't even money to buy vegetables the next day. She was aware that it took very little to drain Hanumanta of all his energy. So she put her head on his chest, apologized to him for having fought with him, and consoled him. It was then that Hanumanta told Shobhi about the pictures and the video that he had seen on Gopal's phone. And about the large sum of money villagers who make such pictures could get. Shobhi, too, did not sleep for the rest of that night.

During that weekend, while Gopal was waiting to board the bus to Pune, Hanumanta asked if he would buy him a mobile phone that had a camera. 'Shobhi is beautiful,' Gopal said, and looked into Hanumanta's eyes with a smile. Hanumanta lowered his eyes. When Hanumanta started taking money out of his pocket, Gopal told him that he could pay him later.

'Super. I'm sure Patil Sahib will like this!' exclaimed Gopal, after he took a look at the pictures and the video on the phone, eyeing Shobhi out of the corner of his eye. She covered her head and her body more tightly with her saree.

A little while later, Patil Sahib came up. Hanumanta and Shobhi rose and bowed.

'Are you the actors?'

Though he did not understand the question clearly, Hanumanta nodded in affirmation.

Patil Sahib pushed Shobhi's saree down from her shoulder and gave her a once-over.

'Hmm. The features are good. We can give a pass mark, right?' Patil Sahib asked Gopal softly as though he were a judge in a beauty contest. Gopal agreed.

'I asked both of you to come to verify that the two people in the video are original. There are many villains who record scenes from other people's bedrooms and bring them over. And if any of these people file a case, we, those that upload this, will be the ones getting into trouble,' Patil Sahib said to no one in particular. 'Anyway, let me look at your piece.'

Hanumanta picked up the mobile phone servilely and handed it over to Patil Sahib. 'Did you record it on this? The clarity will be very low, Gopal. What they ask for now is HD quality. A basic minimum of 10 MB is mandatory. If not, they will not accept it.'

Hanumanta did not understand anything that was said. He guessed fearfully that there was something wrong. Patil Sahib opened the gallery and started looking at the pictures and watching the video. 'Just as I had said, Gopal, these images are not clear; looks as though they were shot in a very dark cave. Look, Gopal, this man appears to be like the old bear in a circus, sitting on a cycle and panting. This can only be classified as comedy. It looks as though someone shaking from fear recorded it. Saw the camera shaking?' Patil Sahib kept commenting as he watched the video. 'Look, Gopal, this woman keeps glancing at the camera every now and then. Even though we know this is consensual, shouldn't it look like it was a spy camera – especially in these times? Yuck! What is this? There is a scar on the upper part of her stomach. Seems like she was wounded by someone. Do you think respectable men will be able to watch and enjoy this, you bandicoot?' Patil Sahib looked angrily at Hanumanta. He lowered his head.

'That scar happened when we had to sell a kidney, Patil Sahib,' Shobhi said softly. 'It was three years ago. An agent promised us three lakhs, and finally gave us just thirty thousand. Our son Shambhu had cancer. We tried to save him with that money, but it did not work out. I lost my kidney, I lost my money, and I lost my son. Only this ghastly scar remained.' She covered her face with her hands and wept.

'The loans we took for his treatment are choking us, Patil Sahib. How on earth can we repay that during this drought? It is not because we like to take these pictures, Sahib…' Hanumanta also wept. But Patil Sahib remained unmoved. 'I don't want this. Take it back. These days it is easy to get bathroom selfies of nubile nymphets in the city.' Patil Sahib walked away in a huff.

'Gopal ji, you will have to help us.' Hanumanta rushed forward and fell at Gopal's feet.

'What Patil Sahib said is right. Who shot this video? If you had told me, I would have come over and shot this well for you. These are all bad pictures. Anyway, I'll try speaking to him once again.' Gopal ran after Patil Sahib who was climbing down the stairs. 'Please give them something – they came all the way…'

Patil Sahib winked. 'She's a good piece. You get that mobile from them, give them a pittance and send them away. I will reward you well.' Patil Sahib laughed. Gopal joined in.

'Patil did not like it at all. He says he does not want it. Just give the mobile back to me. You need not pay me for it. Since you came all the way, I will give you the bus fare. That's all I can do for you.' Gopal took the mobile from them and went down. Hanumanta and Shobhi wiped their faces and followed him. 'Gopal ji … the pictures on the phone…' Hanumanta said anxiously as they climbed down the stairs.

'Don't worry. I'll delete them.' They believed Gopal's promise.

When they reached the ground floor, Patil Sahib placed five soiled hundred-rupee notes into Hanumanta's hand. 'This is because Gopal insisted. Here is another mobile that will give you better picture-quality. What we want is not dried-up donkeys like you and your parched paddy fields. Don't you have young girls living nearby? Get them on camera secretly. I'll give you something that will help you clear your debts.' Hanumanta took the mobile and put it in his pocket without saying a word.

They got a bus very quickly. On that journey, as he stared at the paddy fields covered in darkness, it was his daughter Jani's image that came rushing into his mind time and again. His eyes welled with tears; so did Shobhi's.

EMS and the Girl

THERE WAS A STORY THAT Jose never failed to narrate every time he came home on his annual holiday.

Once he was at a bar in Heathrow Airport, peacefully sipping away, waiting for the flight that was to take him to Trivandrum via Kuwait. Suddenly, someone from the ground crew of an airline company rushed up to him. 'Here you are! We have been calling out for you for so long. Please come. Your flight is ready. Please hurry.' Jose was surprised. He looked at his watch – as he knew it, his flight was scheduled to depart only after another two hours. But this man was adamant. 'Please hurry,' he persisted, 'we are running out of time!' He caught hold of Jose's arm in an attempt to get him to move. Jose looked at his boarding pass once again. Yes, there was more time. Jose tried to explain, 'My flight does not take off now; you must have mistaken me for someone else.' The man, however, was not willing to concede. 'Please come, you are our traveller.' A minor scuffle broke out. He insisted that Jose accompany him. Jose refused to budge. 'You have been drinking – that is why you have no idea of the time,' he said. 'I am not drunk,' Jose protested. In the end, the man, almost in tears, said, 'Aren't you the passenger scheduled to leave for Uganda? Please, please come with me and board your flight.'

'Guess what? Even after I showed him my passport and my ticket, he was not convinced that I was not from Uganda. That's the story of my colour!'

Once again, Jose managed to make us laugh. But as always, this was only the prelude to his new story. Glasses were lined up. The bottle was opened. And Jose began.

'One evening, I was driving back home in a hurry after my trip to the grocery store. The evening was slowly sinking into the night. I had put my son to sleep on the bed, with pillows on either side, and left him alone at home. I needed to get back before he woke up. And I had a lot of work to finish before Sini wrapped up her shift and got home. My speed reflected my tearing hurry. Suddenly I felt that someone was following my car. I soon realized that it was not just a feeling – there were indeed three or four cars trying to overtake mine. They kept shouting and gesturing me to stop. Must be some of those pro-white fanatics. After downing a few pegs or snorting their stuff, they need to get off by piling on a black man. And I was the epitome of the black man. I had been at the unenviable receiving end of such behaviour before. For the same reason, I was not willing to yield. I stepped on it – the race was on, cinema-style. After a death-defying drive on the highway that lasted about thirty minutes, I suddenly veered into a bylane and managed to escape. They could not figure out how I had vanished all of a sudden. They went past me at breakneck speed. Relieved that I had somehow saved my life, I turned around to reverse the car and got the shock of my life. There was a girl crouched low in the back of my car.

'"Hey, who are you? Who are those people? How did you get into my car?"

'Truth be told, I was scared.

'"I'll tell you everything. But please get me to someplace safe." She looked ready to burst into tears. Hardly fifteen, she had Mongolian features. She could be Chinese, Thai or Indonesian. I had no clue when, where or how she had got into the car.

'Her really frightened face revealed that she was in some kind of serious trouble. I did not have the heart to abandon her. Come what may, I decided to take her home. I drove fast, sticking to bylanes and local roads as much as possible.

'"I'll call the police," I told her, relieved that I was finally home.

'"No, please don't," she said. "I'll leave. I just need to make a phone call."

'She tried to call someone for a long time in vain. With each failed attempt, she became more and more anxious. "What will I do now?" she asked with great trepidation.

'"I can either get a taxi for you," I said, "or if you are scared to travel alone, I can drop you. Where do you live?"

'"No. I don't want to go home. If I do, they will hand me over to the same man."

'"To whom?"

'"To the guy who was trying to kidnap me."

'"Why?" I asked anxiously.

'"That is their way of doing things."

'"Oh! Mannarkkad Amme!" I placed my hand on my chest. "Are these really your own folk?"

'I had heard of how girls are pushed into prostitution at a young age in places like Thailand. In this day and age, in this wealthy nation, can things like this happen? It was frightening.

'"Please let me stay here for just this one night. I'll leave in the morning on my own," she implored.

'"Here? You? Who do you think I am? I am a respectable guy staying here with my family. My wife will be back from work soon. If she sees you here – ah! That will be enough. We Indians are not like you," I snapped.

'"Please," she pleaded again.

'"No. I'm sorry. I'll drop you wherever you want right now. Come, let's go."

'"No. I won't come. I have to stay here today." She sat on the sofa.

'"No, no, no," I said firmly. This girl had no idea of my Sini, which is why she was behaving like this.

'"Then I will call the police," she said threateningly.

'"Sure, go ahead, call. That will be better. They will save you from your own family."

'"No, no, Uncle, I will call and tell them that you kidnapped me, brought me here and raped me."

'I was aghast. "What? Me?"

'"Yes, Uncle, you. Will you be able to prove otherwise? How did I reach here? With whom? In whose car? For what? You will tire yourself out answering their questions. I will have only one thing to say: that you kidnapped me and brought me here. If you don't want that, you will have to let me stay here for this one night."

'Good God! Why do I have a way with picking up python-sized problems and wearing them around my neck? What do I do now? If she calls the police, I'll be trapped. They will believe only what the woman says. And if Sini turns up in the midst of all that, I'm finished.

'I decided to switch from threatening to reasoning. I urged that she should not do this to a person who had helped her when she was in great danger. I told her that if Sini walked in now, everything would go south. But she was not willing to compromise in any way. She said that she had absolutely no option but to stay here until her friend arrived.

'In the meantime, my son woke up and started crying. He was four years old. The first thing he'd tell his mother when she came back home would be how he saw a new aunty with me in the house. This girl looked all set to throw me to the dogs. It would have been okay if I had a job or a source of income. If my wife yelled at me, I could have asked her to take a walk. But here, she was the sole breadwinner. I was the househusband who took care of our son, the cooking, the washing, the shopping, and so on. It was not that I could not get a job at a store or a gas station or a supermarket. But I would not even earn enough to pay a nanny to look after our son and do some basic housework. The present arrangement made much more financial sense. While I was romancing her, I never latched on to the fact that Sini had always wanted a man who would dance obediently to her tune. No, I'm not unhappy. One needs to make a heaven out of every hell one falls into. In fact, this is not just my story – most of the Malayali men here live more or less the same life.

'I heard Sini's car pull up outside. I got really worried. I immediately took her to the guest room on the first floor. I requested her to lie low and be absolutely silent so that my life wouldn't fall apart. I locked the door and rushed down. And then, the things I did to keep Sini from going upstairs that night were nothing short of a mind-bending comedy. In spite of all that, Sini said many times that it seems as though there's somebody upstairs, that it feels as though somebody flushed a toilet somewhere … I kept her at bay by at times talking of spirits and scaring her, and at others by telling her that she is perhaps losing it, like her aunt.

'It was after Sini left for work the next morning that I entered the guest room. The girl greeted me by saying that she was dying of hunger. I told her that I'd make her whatever she wanted so long as she left in the morning itself. She agreed, sat in front of the landline and started making calls. But she still could not get through to the number she was trying. Unlike last evening, today, with each failed attempt, I was the person who was getting more and more worked up. She calmly wandered around the house, inspecting everything, commenting that the house was beautiful and that I must be loaded. She walked into the kitchen, made coffee, and then again sat down on the sofa and kept trying the same number repeatedly.

'In the midst of all this, I asked her what her name was.

'"Pacquiao Sayang."

'"What?"

'"Pacquiao. If that is difficult for you, you can call me by my pet name that everyone at home uses – Mee."

'"Good God! What names do these people have? Pacavu! Mee!"

'"Okay. What's your name, Uncle?"

'"My name…" I paused. Doubt assailed my mind. If I revealed my real name, what guarantee did I have that she would not trap me again? She's cunning – better to be careful. I needed to tell her a name that she would never ever recall.

'"My name is Elamkulam Manakkal Sankaran Namboodiripad."

'"Oh my God! What on earth is that? Elamkel Mankel … Compared to this, my Pacquiao Sayang is such an easy name."

'"If it's so difficult, you can use my pet name – EMS."

'"That's good – EMS. That's what I'll call you."

'"Where are you from? Indonesia? Thailand?"

'"I am an American, my dear EMS."

'"No. Where are you from originally? Where are your ancestors from?"

'"Who knows? Even my parents don't know – then how would I?"

'"What really happened last evening?"

'"Oh my God! The phone is ringing!"

'Without responding to my question, she picked up the phone and started talking loudly. She spoke animatedly in her native tongue. There was sorrow, tears, anger and whatnot in her voice. However, when she hung up at the end of a conversation that lasted for almost thirty minutes, she seemed happy. "He will come. In two hours," she said. "He will take me away. Forgive me for having disturbed you, Uncle. I really had no other option."

'I asked her who was coming to pick her up. She said it was her friend and that he would marry her.

'"So you are not going back home?"

'"Yes, I will. After we are married, they will not be able to do anything."

'I asked her repeatedly about what it was that had happened last night. But she cleverly eluded and deflected these questions. After a while, I gave up. All that mattered now was seeing this headache off once and for all.

'After about two hours, a car pulled up near the gate and honked. As soon as she heard it, she was elated.

'"Thank you, Uncle EMS, we'll meet again." She gave me a hug and a kiss, and ran out towards the gate. Through the window, I watched a boy get out of the car and give her a big hug. Brimming with happiness, she got into the car, and they drove away.

'I had no clue about what had happened or what was happening. The totally mysterious incident ended thus. All that was left were a few strange names to toy with when one was doing nothing: Pacquiao, Mee, Sayang.'

'But did this mysterious incident really end like this?' we asked Jose.

Nothing can ever end nowhere. Everything keeps evolving, as it did in this case as well. Glasses were lined up for a second round. The bottle was opened. And the story continued.

~

'Exactly three days went by. On the fourth day, I got a call in the morning. It was an officer from the State Police. I was asked to report at the local police station as soon as possible. "It's an order," he said. I was shocked. I asked what this was about. "Just come down immediately and then you will know," was the response. I dressed quickly, dropped my son off at the play school and reached the station in just thirty minutes. A sergeant took me to the officer's room. He was waiting for me. Without any preamble, he asked me if I had heard of the number 4HIG817 anywhere.

'I did not have to think at all. "That's the number of my car, sir," I said.

'"Who uses it regularly?"

'"I use it."

'"We have received a complaint. About five days ago, an Asian girl was abducted in this car. Do you have anything to say regarding this?"

'I was aghast.

'"Sir, I did not kidnap anyone. She got into my car without my knowledge." I explained everything that happened without missing a single detail. I was almost in tears when I finished narrating the story. The officer got up, came over to my side and patted my shoulder. "You don't have to worry – we just needed to know what exactly happened, that's all. Now tell us, where's she now?"

'"I don't know. She was picked up by her friend in a car and she left."

'"Why did you not report this incident to the police?"

'"She said if I called the police, she would trap me with a false case of sexual assault. I got scared."

'"Even so, don't you know that hiding and abetting a minor is a crime?"

'I remained silent.

'He asked the sergeant to escort someone in.

'First, a young man, and then, a middle-aged man and woman walked into the room.

'One glance at them and I knew that they were relatives of Pacquiao, the bastards who were willing to sell their daughter for money. And now they had filed a case saying that I abducted their daughter?! I felt rage surge through me. If this had happened back home, I would have bashed their teeth in.

'The police officer told them my story in detail. It was the young man who was listening intently. He kept translating it for the other two in their native tongue.

'After they heard the whole story, they started crying. The police officer asked them to leave.

'"Sir, those tears are not real. She told me that she ran away because they were trying to sell her to someone," I said after they had left the room.

'"Trying to sell her?"

'"Yes, sir. I offered to drop her back home, but she refused saying that she was afraid her folk would hand her back to the people who were trying to kidnap her."

'He burst out laughing. "Did she really say that? That may be true, they are Hmongs. Their traditions and customs are really strange."

'I had no clue what he was talking about.

'He saw me off saying that I would be summoned if required in connection with the investigation. He also requested me to cooperate with them until the case was closed.

'I now had another name to toy with: Hmong.'

'And then? Were they able to find her? Did you see her after that?' we asked, unable to stifle our curiosity.

'I'll tell you.' Glasses were lined up for a third round. The bottle was opened again. And the story continued.

~

'It was around that time that my son had a really bad bout of fever. When we took him to the hospital we realized that it was pneumonia. We had to admit him in the hospital for a few days. One day, as I was walking into the hospital, I saw the young man who was present at the police station. The minute he saw me, he came running towards me.

'"Sir, do you remember me? I am Ya Wang. We met at the police station…"

'"Oh yes. You are Pacquiao's brother, right?"

'"No. I am her cousin."

'"Really? Have you heard from her? Do you have any information?"

'"No. We were hoping that we would be able to trace her when we handed over the vehicle number to the police. We are so sorry that we inconvenienced you." He suddenly became very humble and apologetic.

'"No. That's okay."

'"Sir, why are you here?"

'When I told him about my son's illness, he expressed his desire to come with me and see him. I did not dissuade him. He sat with my son for a while and left.

'Two days later, in the afternoon, he landed up in the hospital room with a whole bunch of people. They stood around my son's bed. Caught unawares, I was left with no option but to watch what was happening from a corner in the room.

'An old man in that group inspected my son, as though he were a doctor.

'"Do what you want with me. But please leave my sick son alone," I implored.

'He glared at me and then said something to Ya Wang.

'"Sir, your son is quite unwell. The shaman says that regular treatment will not work."

'Before I could say anything, he started gesticulating with his hands above my son's body, as though he were doing a ritual, all the while chanting something that I could not make neither head nor tail of.

'"There are seven souls in a human body. Two of them have already left your son's body. That is why he is so severely ill. He is trying to bring them back into your son's body," Wang explained to me in private.

'After completing the ritual that lasted for almost fifteen minutes, he spoke to Wang again. Wang translated that for me: "He has prepared the path for the two souls that left your son's body to return. We will now wait for two days. If they don't return and if your son is not on the path to recovery, the shaman will come again to administer a stronger treatment. If required, on that day, to appease the dark elements that have trapped his souls, we might sacrifice a fowl."

'"No. All I want is for all of you to leave." I was almost on the verge of tears.

'After accepting a token payment, he and his people left. However, I did not let Wang leave with them.

'"This shaman? Who's this shaman?"

'"He is the medium who works between the physical and the ethereal world. He is the curer of all ills. His treatment will work even if your allopathy medicine fails. That is his strength."

'"Ha. If so, why haven't you traced Pacquiao yet? Why don't you ask your shaman to locate her using his skills?" I mocked him.

'"He is a healer. He does not have magical skills to locate people who have vanished," he said, in a very low voice.

'I felt bad that I had taunted him. "How are Pacquiao's parents?" I asked, in an attempt to change the topic.

'"They are going through the pain of having lost a daughter."

'"But she does not think very highly of them. Which, in fact, is why she ran away," I said a bit harshly.

'"Which parent will accept the infatuation of a sixteen-year-old? We are Asians, aren't we? Wherever in the world we are, will we forget our culture and ways of approaching things? That's the only way they wronged her – if at all."

'I still did not believe him. People like him will say anything to achieve their ends. They will wax eloquent about the girl child, and yet, if they get an opportunity, they will sell her to a whorehouse. One has heard so many such stories. I decided to interrogate Wang further.

'"She told me that she hid in my car to escape from someone who was trying to kidnap her. Who was this person?"

'"It was me she was trying to escape from. It was me who was chasing your car."

'"You?! You cruel bastard. And now you stand here and weep for her? I will have to tell this to the police."

'"That was not to hurt her. It was because I was in love with her."

'"That does not give you the licence to traumatize a girl. Where were you trying to take her?"

'"You have really misunderstood me. According to our Hmong tradition, if you love a girl, you have to kidnap her and take her to your own house to live with her. And then the two families come together and conduct the wedding. What you call kidnapping here, is, in reality, the sign of love."

'"What? Don't tell me this is how you live in these modern times – that, too, in this country? Doing rituals to cure illnesses? Kidnapping girls in the name of love? Don't you know that the law does not allow all this?"

'"We Hmongs have lost everything. All that is left of what we can call our own are these traditions. Shouldn't we at least preserve them? How else can we sustain our identity?"

'I did not have an answer.

'"Sir, you know that America is the country where the maximum number of girls disappear. And it is young girls like Pacquiao that whorehouses and porn film-makers look for. We desperately need to find her. I'm sure that she will come and see you some day. If that happens, please call me. We want Pacquiao back."

'He gave me his phone number and left.'

'And then? Did she come and meet you ever? Did they find her? Or…?' we asked, unable to contain our curiosity.

'I'll tell you.' Glasses were lined up for a fourth round. A second bottle was opened. The story continued.

~

'No. She never came to meet me.

'In fact, I had almost forgotten about that incident when something happened in America that was widely talked about: an Asian mother killed her four children and committed suicide in Sacramento, the capital of California. This led to widespread discussions on the emotional and mental health of migrants in America. Newspapers and television channels were filled with the opinions of psychologists and psychiatrists. Though almost all media channels referred to her as an Asian mother without disclosing her identity, I came to know from one publication that she was a Hmong. That made me very anxious. I wanted to know who this Hmong was. After several days, I called Wang.

'"What is it, sir? Do you have any information about her?" he asked anxiously.

'"No. But I would like to meet you."

'"You can drop in whenever you want."

'One day, after dropping my son at the school, I went to meet Wang. The address that he had given me took me to a crowded locality in Fresno. It was a street filled with Hmong faces, and it felt like I was in some East Asian country. He was waiting in front of the KFC outlet as he had promised. I parked, and then we walked through the street aimlessly.

'"Which country is this? Indonesia? Thailand? Myanmar?"

'Wang laughed.

'"Like Little India and Chinatown in Long Island, this is the street of the Hmongs in America," Wang said. "There are large settlements like these in Sacramento and Minnesota as well. According to government records, there are three million Hmongs in America. In reality, the number will be much more.

'We walked until Wang stopped in front of a narrow apartment. When he rang the bell, Pacquiao's father opened the door. I had no clue that this was where Wang was headed. I was a bit taken aback. But Pacquiao's father took my hand and led me in. He looked much older than when I had last seen him at the police station. A bunch of kids, more or less of the same age, came out and gathered around him. "Pacquiao's siblings," said Wang. Her mother also came into the room. That apartment seemed completely inadequate for such a large family. The disconcerting stench of poverty pervaded the room.

'"This is Pacquiao's father, Wu Sayang. And this is her mother, Yer Sayang," Wang introduced them. Using the available English at his command, Wu apologized to me, and thanked me for taking the trouble of dropping in. He cried when we started talking about Pacquiao. So did his wife.

'"What was her real problem?" I asked.

'"She was born and brought up here. She knows only the American way of life. And the two of them, in spite of all these years, never really acclimatized to this culture, this language or the food. Isn't that a perfect problem in the making?" Wang replied.

'Pacquiao's mother served coffee. I managed to gulp it down in spite of the faint smell of fish emanating from the cup.

'"I am surprised that the police have not traced her yet," I said, as we walked back.

'"They could have traced her if they wanted to. This is just indifference. We are Hmongs, after all. Who cares?"

'"Who are these Hmongs?" I voiced the question that had been on my mind for a while.

'"The largest community of people in the world who don't have a country to which they belong."

'"I've never heard of such a community of people."

'"Not just you, probably nobody has heard of them. You can hear the voices of Palestine, Bosnia, Sri Lanka, Peru, Chechnya and Tibet anywhere and everywhere. Simply because there are large financial and religious groups behind them. We don't have that. And for the same reason, we don't have a voice that anyone can hear."

'"Which is your motherland?"

'"That's the question that we find most difficult to answer. Every homeless person in the world dreams of going back some day to become a part of the country to which he or she belongs. In fact, very often, this becomes a goal to be realized. But we don't have such a dreamland. Hmongs are people who lived in a province in South China from ancient times. When the Qing dynasty came to power in China in the seventeenth century, we were driven out, and almost all of us had to flee and take refuge in countries like Vietnam, Laos, Thailand and Burma. The largest number of Hmongs took refuge in Laos. History did not allow us to live for long in Laos either. From there we moved to Indonesia. So, if you ask us to which country we belong, we are not sure if the answer should be China, Laos or Indonesia."

'"How then did such a large number of Hmongs end up in America?"

'"It's not just America. We are there in Australia, France, French Guinea, Canada … This is the price that we had to pay for the biggest blunder committed in history – right up to this very day."

'As we neared my car, I stopped and said goodbye to Wang as well as Pacquiao's father who'd chosen to accompany us. As I drove back, I felt the anger and resentment I had been nurturing against them slowly dissolve.

'How on earth did these Hmongs reach America in such large numbers? Who are they, really?' We were suddenly curious about that as well.

'I'll tell you.' Glasses were lined up for a fifth round. The second bottle was opened again. And the story continued.

~

'That trip to Pacquiao's house resulted in Wang and I becoming friends. We'd meet in a restaurant or a park in our corner of California and speak at length about different topics. One day, the famous suicide of the Asian family became the topic of discussion.

'"The situation in America destroyed their belief that they had moved to a country that was heaven on earth. This country gifted them nothing but disappointment. The measure of this disappointment cannot be fathomed easily. One needs to experience it to understand its full import … Why don't we go somewhere today?"

'"Where?"

'"Come, let me take you…"

'We got into the car right away and drove quite a distance on the highway. And then we navigated small roads and bylanes to reach a dense forest on the slope of a hill. There we had to stop the car and walk along a mud trail. It was difficult to believe that there was such a place in America. We finally reached a log cabin. There was an old man there. We gave him the fruits and snacks that Wang had bought en route. I thought they would have a chat, but they did not. We sat in front of him for a while. And then quietly got up and walked back. I decided that, like the shaman, he too must be a yogi or a master, an integral part of the Hmong tradition. But on second thoughts, his face appeared too weary to be that of a yogi.

"'Why didn't you speak with him?" I asked Wang as soon as we were out of the cabin.

"'If the answers are never related to the questions that are being asked, why bother?"

"'I didn't quite get that."

"'He is not in a condition to respond to questions. Soldiers who survive often suffer from depression; he has been a victim of this condition for the last ten years. Leading a solitary life is the way in which he gets some sort of relief. That is why we arranged for him to stay here. We visit him occasionally. That's it. I guess that is what he wants as well."

"'Which was the war that reduced him to this?" I asked him as we drove back.

"'The Vietnam War. It was when America was caught unawares by the war tactics of Ho Chi Minh that they stumbled upon our community on the streets of Laos. And we, people living without a country to seek refuge in, believed that that meeting came in the guise of our salvation. Soon, the CIA recruited all the Hmongs into the

American army. They started a guerrilla unit under the leadership of Major General Vang Pao and assigned Hmongs to lead the war from the front. But how on earth could they battle the soldiers trained by Ho Chi Minh? Tens of thousands of Hmongs perished in the war in Vietnam. But what we actually lost was not the war – we were defeated after the war. We were abandoned on the streets of Laos when America gave up on the war and left Vietnam. The communists, who came in hordes, took out their anger towards the Americans on us. This resulted in a mass exodus of the Hmongs.

"'Thousands were killed. Thousands ran helter-skelter into the villages. Tens of thousands of Hmongs swam the Mekong River and escaped into Thailand. But that, too, was not really an escape. They just moved into another hell, one that reduced them to being refugees and victims of hunger, pain and suffering for several years. After consistent appeals, all the guerrillas in General Vang Pao's army were shipped to America as refugees. It did not take them long to realize that refugees will always be refugees. Their great big American dream began to crumble. To make matters worse, America kept disowning us as well as the Secret War in Laos for many years. It drove everyone who fought bravely in the War to utter despair and disappointment. My papa is one perfect testament."

"'Was that your father we met in the forest?"

"'Yes. Finally, after twenty-two long years, it was the Clinton administration who acknowledged the service of the Hmongs in the Vietnam War. But Papa was too far gone by then. And we did not have the money to pay for expensive treatment here, in America."

'"Wang, what do you do now?"

'"It's not that I'm trying to repeat the stupid mistakes made in our past, but I have applied to enroll in the American army. I know that America still needs Hmongs to be in the frontline of one battle or the other."

'Suddenly there was nothing more to say.'

~

'Was there any information after that about the girl or her family?' we asked Jose.

'No. Not long after that, Wang got a job in China and he left. And our relationship petered out. I did enquire about the girl's family. America had implemented a programme to return Hmongs to various settlements in Laos. What I understood was that they went back to Laos as part of this programme.'

Sensing that the story had come to an end, we emptied our glasses and started getting up. The next time round, there would be a new story, a new spirit, a new get-together.

It was then that Jose's wife Sini came in. 'Why is everyone looking so out of sorts after listening to Jose's story? Anyway, he has only one story to tell every time, right? The story of the ground crew at the Heathrow Airport,' Sini teased him. 'You guys must be really bored of hearing the same story again and again. This time, I'll tell you an interesting story.'

'Sini? Story? Okay. We're all ears.'

Glasses were lined up for a sixth round. A third bottle was opened. We sat down again to listen to Sini's story.

~

'Last Christmas, Jose travelled home to India alone. This was something that happened then. It was winter and it was snowing. One morning, when I came home after my night shift, someone was sleeping on the steps outside the door. I was frightened. I got out of the car and ran in, only to discover that it was a girl. She looked really bedraggled, scrawny and tired. As soon as she saw me, she asked me a really strange question: "Is EMS here?"

'"EMS? Who's that?"

'"The owner of this house, Mr Elamkulam Manakkal … he used to live here."

'EMS – that sounded very familiar. Wasn't he a politician from Kerala? How could he be in my house? I became suspicious.

'"Are you talking about the Indian EMS?"

'"Yes, yes. I once stayed with him here."

'To be honest, I felt like laughing out loud. She was either mad, or she was teasing me. Whatever it may be, I decided that I would not give in.

'"Why do you want to meet him?"

'"I want to request him to help me with something. I reached here with great difficulty late last evening and rang the bell, but nobody answered. And I had nowhere else to go to. Which is why I decided to sleep here, on these steps."

'"Oh, you poor thing. I've heard that he is a man who helps everyone. But unfortunately, he passed away last year in Kerala. Did you have anything to tell him?" I teased.

'"He died? Was he ill?"

'"No idea. He died, that's it."

'She left the house in tears.

'How's that for you? Crazy she might be, but even a girl in America came in search of EMS from Kerala when she had a problem. Imagine – EMS in America! That, too, in my house!' Sini burst into laughter. But none of us felt like laughing. Sini became quite angry.

'Why are you guys not laughing? Will you laugh only at Jose's Heathrow story? You guys better laugh: EMS in America – that, too, in Jose's house!'

We laughed aloud with Sini.

The Postman

SADASHIVAN PILLAI, OUR POSTMAN, DIED last week.

Although it had been thirteen long years since he had retired, in our minds he continued to be the postman. And though there were many a replacement that cycled into his role, insofar as we were concerned, none of them could really replace Sadashivan Pillai. For the same reason, the people of this land saw him off to the next world with great respect. That evening, under the initiative of the citizens' forum, there was a large condolence meeting at the market junction. Though everyone turned up, though the postman used to live just ten houses away from mine, and though I was doing nothing but leafing through magazines, I did not go for this meeting. Rather than attend funerals for the sake of duty or formality, I had decided that I would bid farewell to only those people who had had a significant impact on my life. There is a reason why I am telling you this now.

One morning, last week, when I was seated in the verandah reading the newspaper, very unusually, Vijayakumar, the postman's son, dropped in. Though we had studied together in the same classroom in school for five years, we were not friends enough to exchange pleasantries when we met on the road, or in Yesudas's tea shop. After high school, he got into the Industrial Training Institute, trained to be an electrician, and soon joined the Kerala State Electricity Board as a lineman. I, on the other hand, studied history and economics, whiled away my time looking for a job, and when I was on the verge of thirty, bid adieu to my big dreams and ended up being a librarian in a private college in town. In reality, there was actually nothing in our lives that we could share with each other. For the same reason, his arrival in the morning perturbed me a bit – but without revealing it, I welcomed him, asked him to sit, and hollered into the house for another cup of tea.

'Was the postman bedridden?' I decided that this would be the best way to start the conversation.

I felt that my question was a welcome relief to Vijayakumar, who seemed to be at a loss to know where to begin.

'No, he was fine. He had dinner and went to bed. A bit later he asked for water; he drank it, hiccupped once and closed his eyes. It was really an effortless passing.'

With one simple sentence Vijayakumar successfully did away with the opportunity to prolong a conversation about illness, how even our vegetables are sprayed with poison, hospital expenses, the angst of being a caregiver, and a host of possibly related topics.

'He's lucky. He was a good man,' I said, using simple commonsense to tie things up.

All of a sudden, Vijayakumar took a card out of his pocket and gave it to me. I thought it was the invitation to the fifth-day ceremony, the Sanjayanam.

'Some Basheer sent this to you. I found this yesterday, when I was going through my father's bag. For someone who was really meticulous, I don't know how he forgot this. Anyway, I thought it was my duty to hand this over to you before the Sanjayanam.'

I was very curious. There was no Basheer I knew who could have sent me a postcard.

It was when I looked at the card that I got a shock. It was not 'some' Basheer who had sent that postcard. It was the one and only Vaikom Muhammad Basheer. 'May God bless you', said the card, with his full signature below it. Suddenly, like a bat darting out of the dark recesses of my mind, I remembered sending him a letter in the excitement of having read his *Balyakalasakhi* a very, very long time ago. Was this the reply to that letter? From the thin seal on the faded postcard, I managed to read the date – it was sent exactly one year before Basheer passed away. After twenty long years of hibernation, the postcard had finally reached me. This is probably a first in the entire world: an ardent admirer receiving a reply from a writer two entire decades later. But unfortunately, it was way past the age and the time for it to have created the high excitement it once would have. From being an aficionado of books and writers, I was now reduced to being their watchman. No letter – from Basheer or any other writer – could give me that shot in the arm any more. I folded the postcard and put it in my pocket dispassionately.

'Even before he retired, he had started forgetting things. That's probably what happened. Please don't tell this to anyone.' Vijayakumar's voice was laced with the guilt of the postcard having been delayed by twenty years. I admired his honesty. 'No, it's okay,' I reassured him. 'What matters is that you did not have the heart to just tear it up.'

'You know how much my father was feared by the people here. We, at home, were more scared of him. None of us even had permission to step into his room.' Suddenly, Vijayakumar got up to leave. As he walked out, he ignored my request to have a cup of tea.

I mused about what Vijayakumar had said and realized that it was true. Though the title 'Postman' did not evoke fear – as would 'Policeman' or 'Judge' – everyone there was a bit scared of Postman Sadashivan. If *exacting* had a synonym, it would be him. People who had too much hope and too little patience had a habit of clustering around the post office in the morning to collect their letters. It was Sadashivan Pillai who put an end to that. He would ignore the whole lot and just cycle away with everything they wanted in his mail bag.

Sadashivan Pillai had an explanation for this: 'The government does not pay me to break the law, stand on the steps of the post office, call out names and distribute letters.

The government pays me to deliver every single letter to the right address.'

En route, if someone were to ask him if there was mail, the person would be gifted with a look that would singe, delivered with one foot on the pedal and the other on terra firma. And on reaching a residence, he would be adamant that he would hand over the letter only to the person to whom it was addressed – especially if it was a money order, a registered letter or a parcel.

If any housewife were to make the mistake of saying, 'Kochetten has gone to tether the cow in the backyard. Just hand the letter to me, Pillecha, I'll give it to him,' he would retort gruffly, 'Why, will Kochetten stay in the backyard the whole day?', and then stand there in the front yard and smoke until Kochetten showed up. His parting shot after handing over the letter would be: 'Next time, if you want me to hand the letter over to your dearly beloved, please come to the post office and submit a written request.'

So, when every other postman would complete their rounds by three and get back to the post office, I have seen Sadashivan Pillai doing his rounds on the cycle even at six in the evening.

Sadashivan Pillai had an explanation for this as well: 'The postman has a duty to his land – to deliver letters on time, all the while protecting the privacy of the addressee. As long as I have this job, I will do this, irrespective of what time of the day or night it is.'

There were a few people who really liked the fact that the postman was disciplined and strict:

1. Chambakathadathil Malini was one of them, because he would deliver the love letters that came for her without handing them over to her father.
2. Eruthikkavil Gomathi Chechi, because he would hand over the money order from her son only to her and not to the demoness-in-law.
3. Mulankavil John-etten, because he would deliver the repayment card from the bank directly to him and not say a word to anyone including his own family about the loan that John-etten had secretly taken for Janamma who worked for the cooperative society.

The list went on.

Across his tenure that spanned twenty-seven years, the recognition for best service came looking for Sadashivan Pillai thrice. Though some people called it an award for making life difficult for the common man, it was only when he retired and the new postman took over that people realized the value of Sadashivan Pillai. Letters started getting lost regularly because they were entrusted to neighbours and passersby, which, in turn, triggered many a squabble; letters were delivered to the wrong people: the letter to Janaki Chechi reached Ponnamma

Chitta, Pappanabhan's money went to Rajendran; and many a letter, by virtue of being flung over the gate like a newspaper, ended up literally being washed away by the rain.

It was then that Sadashivan Pillai, regarded mostly as an enemy, was elevated in the minds of the people as the real postman who deserved great respect. Across the next thirteen years, stories of his punctuality, his honesty, and his dedication to work became the stuff of legend. A few old men sitting in front of Pakkaran Pillai's small shop-that-sells-everything kept telling themselves that a few more men like Sadashivan Pillai were needed in the community. Youngsters, when they saw the postman on his way to the market to buy tapioca and fish, would show him their respect by removing the headphones from their ears. The loud, abusive bunch of people outside the bar would lower their voices and disperse when they saw him. People who bickered at the village assembly would keep quiet in his presence.

So, why on earth had the postman, now revered by everyone for his discipline and exactitude, kept the postcard that he should have handed over to me twenty years ago? Was it because of his respect for Basheer? Or was it something else that I could not fathom? This question kept haunting me.

Days later, Vijayakumar dropped in again. His uniform, one that stank of sweat, told me that he was on his way back from work.

'I did not see you for the Sanjayanam,' Vijayakumar complained as he stepped into the verandah. Although 'but you never invited me' was on the tip of my tongue, I cooked up a befitting excuse on the spur of the moment. I did not tell him that I normally refrain from attending not just funerals but also Sanjayanams.

'I need to tell you a secret,' said Vijayakumar, after a few initial inconsequential exchanges were over. My eyebrows asked him what it was. He asked me to step out with him, which I did.

'There is something that has been seething within me for many days now. I thought a lot about whether I should speak to someone about it or not. I've got to a point where if I don't share this with someone, I'll probably burst. But the question was whom could I share it with? There are people everywhere but nobody who would understand this.'

We stepped on to the road and ambled towards the Vayarappuzha river. A couple of familiar faces who were walking towards us stared at the unfamiliar pair.

'Remember, I had handed over a postcard to you, the one that I got from my father's bag? To be honest, it was not just one card that belonged to you that was in my father's bag. Over time, my father had kept many letters addressed to different people in his bag instead of handing them over. It's not just one or two letters – it's a box full of them!'

I was really stunned. This was something that you'd never think Postman Sadashivan would do – not even in your wildest dreams. Squirrelling away letters in his bag instead of handing them over to the various addressees. This was definitely not forgetfulness, this was an intentional offense.

'I just cannot understand how someone as responsible as Achan could do something like this, knowing fully well that it was wrong. I really don't know what to do with those letters. At times I think the best thing to do would be to quietly burn them all without anyone seeing. Then I think that it would be better to hand them over to the addressees and correct Achan's mistake. I am increasingly getting a bit scared. I thought I'd ask you for your opinion.'

I had not digested the situation well enough to give him a reply then and there. Nor was I at peace to evaluate what was right and wrong. I was perhaps more lost in the darkness than Vijayakumar was in his predicament. I had only my silence to offer.

'Can I do one thing? Until we arrive at a decision, can I leave the box in your house? A lot of relatives keep moving in and out of his room. Achan's sisters, my sisters and brothers – they are all hunting high and low for his will. If someone stumbles across this box, I am certain that they will make it public and try to taint his name.'

I continued to remain silent.

'After everyone has slept tonight, I will come over and signal you with a torch. Just come out and take the box from me.'

Though it all seemed right out of a ridiculous detective novel that I had read in the distant past, I accepted the box from Vijayakumar that night and hid it in the empty corner of the cupboard on the first floor.

It stayed there for almost three weeks. Amid the bustle of everyday life, I forgot about the box. And Vijayakumar never turned up to remind me either. And then, one weekend, when my wife and children went off to visit her parents, the box suddenly popped into my mind. Right or wrong, I decided to go up and take a look at the letters.

In my first, quick, eager scan itself, I realized that the letters spanned the entire twenty-seven long years of the postman's career. I also realized that Vijayakumar's idea of handing over the letters to many of the addressees would not be possible. Many of them had already vanished under the blanket of time.

The box contained envelopes with large stamps from the Gulf, a notification of a gas connection, money orders, drafts which had expired long ago, seizure notices, intimations of death, appointment orders, wedding cards, public meeting notices, musical birthday cards, new year cards, love letters…

As I was traversing through this small mountain of letters, I came across a really old, thin, pink diary. At first I thought that it was a gift for someone that the postman had decided to intercept; but when I leafed through it, I realized that it contained the postman's own notes.

This was the note on the first page:

> A postman is not just a person who delivers letters. He is someone who understands the pulse of a land, someone who can read the minds of its people. There is a time within which a letter should reach its addressee. If a letter arrives ahead of its time, it might derail the life of the person who receives it. It will rewrite their destiny. It will be impossible for a postman who believes in justice to be party to that. Hence, it is the duty of a good postman to ensure that certain letters do not reach their destination. A man knowingly does something wrong because he believes, in his own way, deep down inside, that it is the right thing to do. I hope that in the future, what I considered right is proven to be what time also considered right.

The following pages contained explanations of why each letter was not delivered to the respective addressee.

1. I am certain that this envelope contains the draft that Prabhakaran sent from Persia. But his wife, Padmaja, is too much of a spendthrift. There is no end to the money she spends on clothes and cosmetics. The money that Prabhakaran makes by sweating it out in the desert should not be squandered thus.

2. I am not handing over this seizure notice to Kunjappichayan for the time being. He already has a heart problem. He is running around to get his daughter married. This notice will not do them any good right now. Let his daughter's marriage get over. By then the bank will send the second notice.
3. He is one of the few youngsters in this town who reads books. If a postcard from such a renowned writer reaches him now, there is a very good chance that he will become too full of himself. Let him read more and become mature enough to face life stoically. I will then gift him this card.

I realized that he was referring to the card that Basheer had sent me. Then why was it that he never handed over the card to me? Did he put it in his box and forget all about it? Or was it because he never felt that I was mature enough?

That whole night, I went through the letters that had been imprisoned by the postman's idea of justice.

Vijayakumar dropped in again.

'Did you tell anyone?' he asked anxiously as soon as he walked in.

'If you had no faith in me, you should not have handed them over to me,' I said a bit emotionally.

'No, it's not that. I'm unable to sleep. The only thing he gifted us was his good name. The value of saying that I am the postman's son is priceless. I am just worried that my carelessness will ruin it all.'

'I went through the letters a few days ago. I did not find any letter that will be of use if delivered now. The best thing to do for you and the postman will be to burn them.'

'You think so? All this time I have been worrying about the number of lives that would have taken a different turn because of my father's misdeeds. There's nothing like that, right?' Vijayakumar asked, as if to console himself.

'No. There's nothing like that. Not only that, but a lot of people also continued to live peacefully just because those letters never reached them.'

'So, what my father did was not that big a crime, was it?'

'No, not at all.'

'Then let us burn them all now. I will never be at peace as long as they exist in this world.'

I agreed. Between the two of us, we gathered all the letters and burned them in my backyard. When they were reduced to ashes, Vijayakumar sighed, hugged me, and walked away.

I hoped that his peace would keep him safe. But there was something he did not know: I had removed one set of letters and tucked them into the drawer of my table.

That night, as I went through the letters, I found a small bundle held together by a rubber band. I took the rubber band off and was surprised to find who they were all addressed to: Girija Teacher, who taught me in the upper primary school. The sender's address was not stated in any of those letters. What was really curious was not that, but that all the letters were numbered in a sequence. There were twenty-two letters in that bundle, numbered 243 to 264. There was no way of finding out if the sender had numbered it or the postman.

There was another thing that worried me. In that entire box, there were not more than two letters addressed to the same person. So why did he not deliver twenty-two letters to Girija Teacher? I went through the postman's diary once again to find out if there was any mention of these letters, but there were none. He had an explanation for having intercepted every letter, but there was no explanation given for these twenty-two letters.

Although I was often tempted to open at least one of these letters, the sheer burden of the secret it might contain dissuaded me. Especially since I knew Girija Teacher well. She taught me social science from the fifth to the seventh standard. I have often told many people that it was her classes that inspired me to get a postgraduate degree in the same subject. Her classes were that good.

Our relationship with Girija Teacher was not limited to the classroom. Often after school, we would walk with her to her house, which stood on a really large plot that was full of trees laden with fruit – water apple, guava, scramberry, chikoo … That was fertile, unrestricted grazing ground for brats like us. Hunger and greed satiated, we would return to find Girija Teacher's husband Gopi Sir sitting in his armchair on the lawn. He would entertain us by telling us stories, reciting poems and giving us riddles to solve. Those evenings were joyful journeys for us. But it was much later, along the way, that we realized that Gopi Sir was progressing into a world that was slowly turning pitch black – he was going blind.

It had been a long time since I had seen Girija Teacher. I did not even know if she was still alive. Although I expected her to be on the dais along with the other teachers on the hundredth anniversary of the school, she was not there. After I got this treasure trove of letters, I felt that I should go see her. When I met headmaster Anandan Sir at the temple, I enquired about Girija Teacher. 'I rarely see her out anywhere these days. I think she is not well,' he said casually.

The next day, on the way back from work, I dropped in at Girija Teacher's house. It was no longer a house filled with light and laughter. Darkness seemed to have fallen over it. She had great difficulty in recognizing me. Even after she did, her face did not light up with that old smile. She replied to all my pleasantries and questions, mostly in monosyllables. Amidst all that, I managed to figure out that Gopi Sir had passed away about nine years ago. I took leave of her when I realized that my forays into the past would never bring that old smile back to her face.

I came back home, went upstairs and took those letters out – the twenty-two letters that had never reached her. Why did the postman not deliver these? What would have been the reason? Did the postman know who sent these letters? Did he know what was in these letters? Did the postman know how these would affect Girija Teacher's life? Or did the postman yield to any ulterior motive?

That night, all these thoughts crawled through my mind incessantly like ants, robbing me of my sleep. But by morning, I had taken a decision. I took the first letter from the lot, placed it in another envelope, wrote Girija Teacher's address on it and put it in the post box. The letter, whose journey was interrupted for mysterious reasons many years ago, was once again on its way to the rightful recipient. From then on, I started sending her the remaining letters one by one, with an interval of four to five days in between.

On the day I posted the seventh letter, I bumped into Anandan Sir on the way back from work. I told him about my visit to Girija Teacher's house and her current state of health.

'I actually did not tell you all that,' said Anandan Sir. 'I think the real disease that spread darkness across the last few years of Gopi Sir's life was suspicion. Teacher suffered a lot during that time.'

I did not feel like probing further. Nor did Anandan Sir say anything else. For some reason, a sadness crept over my mind. I went straight to Girija Teacher's house on my scooter. Unlike the last time, there was a light glowing in the verandah. I stood there for a while. I thought I heard someone singing in a feeble voice inside the house. Soon I realized that it was indeed someone singing. A shiver ran through my spine. Although I had come all the way to see

Girija Teacher, I turned away without going in and drove back home.

Though I posted the rest of the letters in the coming days, I did not go to Girija Teacher's house again – I was afraid to.

One day, after I had posted the last letter, on the way back from work, I met Vijayakumar. Amidst all the chatter, he told me one thing.

'Do you remember Girija Teacher who taught us social studies? She came home a few days ago. It was only recently that she came to know of Achan's passing. She sat and spoke to me for a long time. What was really surprising was that as she was about to leave, she hugged me and broke into tears. Poor thing. Wonder what overwhelmed her…'

Vijayakumar looked at me as though for a response. I shook my head. But I told something to myself: 'I can fill up the blank pages in the postman's diary now.'

Vijayakumar turned around as though I had said something. But I drove away on my scooter without looking at him.

Javed the Mujahideen

I

THE AUTHOR'S STORY

IF OUR DAILY ROUTINE IS upset even slightly, we get perturbed, don't we? Which is probably why, at that point, we are willing to befriend someone very quickly, just to pour our woes out. For instance, when the power fails once in a blue moon in our colony, even if it is for a short while, why should everyone get so upset as if their lives have come to a grinding halt? And run around as though nothing will ever be set right again? You should have seen the state that Mohan Roy – the guy who's sitting and talking to me peacefully now – was in, just a while ago. That was a sight to see.

It must have been about ten minutes since the power failed. That's when Mohan Roy walked in crying, 'Somebody in the colony said that you work with the electricity board. Can't you do something about this immediately, my friend?' He was truly at his wits' end.

This guy, Mohan Roy, stays four villas away from mine. I think he's a senior officer in some company. Our relationship, until then, was limited to the occasional 'hi' or 'bye' in the parking lot.

'The emergency maintenance team was here. The main cable is singed. They will fix it,' I said lightly.

'Yes, I did ask them. They went away saying that the cable has to be changed and that it will take time. Don't know when they'll come back. As an engineer, you could perhaps do something at once … The heat is really stifling.'

Mohan Roy had a truly tragic look on his face. But I knew that there was no point in hurrying. It was the main cable to the colony that was damaged. The external contractual team would have to come, dig up the earth, remove the burnt cable, lay the new one and connect it all up – it would definitely take time.

Though I wanted to explain all this to Mohan Roy, seeing him standing there, looking at me as though he had finally found someone who could set things right, I did not have the heart to.

In the meantime, the entire colony had congregated, like agitated bees, on the road outside their homes. Most of them were getting ready to get into their cars and go elsewhere. Some of them looked like refugees, carting food, clothes, dhurries, blankets, swimming trunks and whatnot. They were planning to go to a cooler place: a hotel, the beach, a cinema, a friend's apartment … The rest were huddled in small groups, talking.

Mohan Roy sat down in my verandah. 'Are you also going somewhere?'

I was on the phone trying to reach a friend.

'Sheesh! If you too leave, I don't think there's any hope of this being fixed and the power coming back tonight. This comes under the purview of your department…'

Mohan Roy looked really disappointed. 'At least you people have a friend's flat to go to. What will we do?'

I wondered how long he'd been staying here. Maybe ten years? Why did he not have a single friend in all these years? What a life!

Mohan Roy must have understood what I was thinking. 'I was not like this, my friend. I came here and I lost everything. It's like I've fallen into this black hole where life has only two dimensions: work and home. I don't know why I gave up a good life to come and live in this furnace.'

I did not pay much attention to all that he said. This was the common bleat of almost everyone who landed up here. A bleat that by now always fell on deaf ears.

But I simply could not bring myself to abandon him in the state that he was in and just go off to my friend's flat.

'Okay. I'll stay put – they might complete the work faster that way.'

'Yes, yes, that is what even I think.' Mohan Roy was happy.

My wife called me in to bicker: 'Why should we stay here and suffer the heat for someone like him who's never even as much as glanced in our direction all these years?'

I explained his helplessness and calmed her down. She contained her disapproval well and served Mohan Roy a glass of juice. He downed it in one go. I then saw a Mohan Roy who was rid of his great burden of stress. He somehow seemed to think that it was all safe in my hands. And then he started to talk as though we had known each other for aeons. I saw a city-dweller in him – one who was deprived of and ached for friends, friendship, conversations, light banter in the evenings, occasional get-togethers … He continued to speak like a man who was hungry and craving expression. It almost seemed as if everything that he wanted to say for centuries had been bottled up inside him. He started with the power failure, then spoke about the city, how busy the city was, his job, how busy the job kept him, and so on and so forth. The long shadow of disappointment in having allowed this mirage of a city lure him here was evident through and through. It was when he moved the conversation from the city to the community that he, very unexpectedly, told me a story.

Yes, he actually told me a story. I was all ears. There are a few writers who are blessed. They have the phenomenal skill of taking a regular event in life and turning it into a brilliant story. But in spite of keeping my eyes and ears open, it was very rarely that I got the right setting for a story. Then the only other option is to tell a second-hand story. In other words, make someone else's experience my own and tell the story. If I hear that someone is going to narrate a story or an experience, I will give up everything and sit down to listen to it, in the hope that it might become the source of my next story. It was with the same feeling that I sat down to listen to Mohan Roy's story.

2

THE STORY THAT MOHAN ROY TOLD

I was in Nainital for a long time, in connection with my work. It was a long time ago. Much before Uttarakhand was formed. Nainital was part of Uttar Pradesh. Though I am basically a Malayali, I was born and brought up in Delhi. I did my Masters in Jawaharlal Nehru University – JNU. As soon as I got out, I got a good job. Junior Lecturer at the renowned St. Joseph's College in Nainital. My subject was political science. Why don't you ask me, my friend, why I left Delhi and went that far? I'll tell you. The girl I wanted as my life-partner – right from high school – was, by then, working in the military as a nurse, with the rank of a Major. She kept insisting that I be there, with her. Who would give up the opportunity to walk with one's beloved through the misty hills of Nainital? Will you give that up, engineer? So, I was in Nainital for a long time – both before and after my marriage. During those days, I knew a guy called Javed Iqbal.

On one of those rare occasions, I met up with Smitha – that's my wife, by the way – outside the campus. We went for a boat ride. This Javed whom I just mentioned, was our boatman. He was probably just about twenty years old. Looked like one of the chocolate heroes of Hindi cinema. Long, slightly crooked nose, and a smile plastered constantly on his face. He was very excited when he came to know that we were from Delhi.

'Where in Delhi? When are you going back to Delhi? Do you know AIIMS? I've come there once. A relative of mine studies there...' He was full of questions, full of doubts.

All this was before we got married. The secret trysts. The magnetic attraction. Delightfully cold Nainital. Beauty all around. Love that makes the heart heavy. Suddenly, as though to provide the right background, Javed started to sing. '*Aapki nazron ne samjha, pyaar ke kabil mujhe; dil ki ae dhadkan theher ja, mil gayi manzil mujhe...*' Oh! You know Lata ji's song, don't you? It makes me cry even today. Such meaningful lines, my friend ... All it took was just that one song to make me an admirer of Javed. But, you know, he sang one song after another for us that day. Rafi, Kishore, Manna Dey, Saigal, Mukesh, Pankaj Mullick ... The songs just flowed as though music were coursing through his veins. With each song, I became more and more convinced that he was not meant to be a mere oarsman, but a great ghazal singer. And I told him so too.

Before we parted that day, I gave Javed the address of my rented house. 'Drop by when you are free in the evenings, Javed. I am new to Nainital – you can tell me your stories and then, perhaps, we can listen to a bit more of Lata in that beautiful voice of yours.' He smiled in agreement.

St. Joseph's was a Catholic institution. After having enjoyed the freedom of JNU, this was like a Nazi camp to me. I was hoping that my search for a friend outside the stifling campus would end with Javed. But contrary to my expectations, Javed never stopped by. And I, too, forgot all about him.

But out of the blue, I met him again one day in the State Bank situated in one of the narrow streets of Bhotia Bazaar. I had gone there to send off an urgent demand draft. He smiled and came up to me. My greeting was lukewarm, and he understood why.

'Travellers feign affection and tell us many things: come to the room, I'll give you a gift, I'll give you money, and so on and so forth. Very often, if you believe them and go meet them, what they actually want is something else. They think we'll pimp our own sisters. Mohan Saab, I knew that you are not like that. It's just that everyone in our line of work jointly decided that we would not accept such invitations. I know that good people like you will be upset. Please don't feel bad,' explained Javed.

'Javed, unlike what you think, I did not come here seeking the pleasures of Nainital. I, too, came here to work, just like you. I'll never trouble you with such requests. Here, I have someone I love to sleep with.' I laughed. So did he.

I think Javed began to trust me. Unexpectedly one evening, he came to my rented house. We cooked and ate aloo-chapati and dal fry together. Until late into the night, we sang the songs of Lata ji, Saigal, Kishore, Mukesh and Rafi. It was a beautiful evening.

That was the beginning. Javed visited me often after that. Each time, we would sing for hours. We would have dinner together. At times he would sleep over. We travelled all over Nainital together: the Nanda Devi National Park, the Valley of Flowers National Park, Snow View Point, China Peak and the Jim Corbett National Park. He filled me in on the entire history and folklore of Nainital.

'You were not meant to be just an oarsman, Javed. Why can't you be a guide? Or something even better?' I asked him.

'Every man has his own destiny, Mohan Saab. We think of going one way, Allah chooses another way. Allah wanted me to be an oarsman, that's it.'

He drowned the remaining questions I was aching to ask with a disarming smile.

He never said anything about his home or his family. A couple of times, when I took the conversation in that direction, he deftly avoided the questions. After that, I did not persist.

And then, suddenly, one day, Javed went missing. I had no clue where he'd gone. I thought he might be sick and laid up. My enquiries at the boat club did not yield any result. No one knew where he was. Many days later, when I went to the bank, it was the bank officer, who, by then, had become an acquaintance of mine, who told me what had happened. 'Did you hear? That boatman who wandered around with you – what's his name? Ah, Javed – he was arrested by the police!'

I was shocked. 'For what?'

'For what? My friend, he was a terrorist from Kashmir. A mujahideen. The swine! Thank God he was caught before something happened. The police investigation has just started. We'll have to wait and see how many people masquerading as angels get caught.' That was the time Kashmir had started burning. News of occasional bomb blasts, kidnapping and revolt had just started surfacing. Was Javed one of them? Was he scheming and plotting while travelling and dining with me? Had he made me his pawn, his cover? If yes, God! Will Smitha and I get entangled into this? How far will the long arm of law reach? A strange dread crawled over me.

'It was my eye for detail that trapped him,' the bank officer said with pride. 'He used to come here regularly to take demand drafts. When I looked closely, they were all made out to Kashmir. I just informed the police of my suspicion. He was picked up the very next day.'

I felt lightheaded. I got out of the bank and started walking.

Kashmir! What did Javed have to do with Kashmir? He had never mentioned any relationship with Kashmir.

Even I, an intelligent, perceptive man from JNU had failed to read him. What kind of avatars will these terrorists take?

I spent several days scared that the police would knock on my door at any time. Just as I had feared, they arrived one day. They questioned me for hours. Most of the questions were about Javed. He had told the police that I was his best friend. I told them everything that had happened since the day I met Javed. In the end, they left saying that they would be back for more information.

But for some reason, they never came again. They must have been convinced that I was telling the truth.

After that, for about four years, I had no news of Javed. In the meantime, I married Smitha. We had a son. I was immersed in submitting a thesis. I forgot the chapter called Javed.

One evening, when I was about to step out of the house, very unexpectedly, I found Javed standing at my door. It was not the young man brimming with energy that I once knew. It was as though he had hit middle age all of a sudden. Truth be told, I was shocked. He understood that instantly.

'How come you've come this way after such a long time?' I asked, as though I did not know anything.

'I came to ask for Saab's help. I need some money urgently. I'll return it as quickly as possible.'

'Why? Is it to help some Kashmiris?' asked Smitha, who, by then, was standing next to me.

He was stunned. But he composed himself quickly. 'Why, Memsaab, is a Kashmiri someone whom the entire world hates?'

'Javed, I'll give you all the money you want,' I said with folded hands. 'But you'll have to do me a favour: never ever come here to meet me again.'

'Why, Saab?' He was visibly upset.

'I'll tell you the truth. Javed, I am scared of Kashmiri mujahideens.'

He laughed out loud – the laughter was laced with a disturbing self-reproach.

'Mujahideen? Me? If I were one, Mohan Saab, I would never have lost my Baba. I would never have had to live the life of an oarsman here. Even the Indian military who caught me released me because they found that I was innocent. But Mohan Saab, you, who know me so well ... It's okay, Saab. This is the fate of a Kashmiri.'

He sat down, weary. And then, for a while, he cried silently. We did not know what to do. Then he got up slowly and asked me if I could walk a bit with him. We walked together, and eventually, reached the lake. We did not speak a word on the way. Javed got into his boat. So did I. He rowed wordlessly for a while. And then, he told me his story.

3

THE STORY THAT JAVED TOLD

I am a Kashmiri. From the time I can remember, my Baba, Sheikh Iqbal Hassan, was a boatman of a shikara on the Dal Lake. I have five younger siblings – three sisters and two brothers. We were a happy family. With tourists coming to the Dal Lake round the year, we were able to live decently well. My childhood, spent in the peaceful Kashmir Valley, is still fresh in my mind, like a rainbow that becomes one with infinity. I was good at studies. I came first in every class. Baba's biggest dream was to make me a doctor. For a boatman on the Dal Lake, that was too big a dream. Actually, it was not Baba's dream. It was a decision made by Dr Anand Shivpuri, someone all of us respectfully called Doctor ji. Right since childhood, it was Doctor ji who guided me and supervised my studies.

'Sheikh Bhai, our Javed is not someone who should end up being a boatman in the Kashmir Valley. So long as this Anand Shivpuri is here, you won't have to worry about his education. I will send him to Delhi. He will come back as a doctor.' This is what he used to tell Baba.

Baba and Doctor ji were soulmates – it was a relationship that defied explanation. If Doctor ji said something, Baba would never contradict that. I've heard Baba say this many a time.

4

THE STORY THAT SHEIKH IQBAL HASSAN TOLD

Son, we then used to live in a small village called Fulwara, on the other side of the Jhelum River that flows through the Kashmir Valley: a distant village with no roads or transportation. How Doctor ji came to that village is a story in itself. A long time ago, when you were hardly two years old, a fever spread across our village. People started to collapse because of high fever and diarrhoea. Initially, we managed to get medicines from the hospitals in the Kashmir Valley. But nothing worked. Children and the elderly began to die. We became really anxious. There was no way we could transport the sick to the hospital. Nor did we have sufficient manpower. Other than a few young people like us, the entire village was ailing. To make matters worse, the Jhelum was overflowing. Our village was more or less flooded. In the hope that we might find a doctor who would be willing to come to the village and treat the people, a couple of us scouted all the hospitals in the Kashmir Valley. We told them about our village and the raging fever, and begged them to visit. But nobody had the courage to cross the overflowing Jhelum. It was when we were almost reconciled to the disappointing conclusion that it was perhaps Allah's decision that our village should be wiped out from this fever, that a young man agreed to come with us. This was Dr Anand Shivpuri, who eventually became an integral part of our village.

I still remember the day he came to our village. I remember taking the shikara out into the angry Jhelum. We had to travel three kilometres downstream to reach the other side. Water had drowned many parts of the village. The rain was incessant. With his leather bag full of equipment and medicines, he waded and at times swam from one house to another to treat the sick. He gave them shots and medicines. We had to carry him on our shoulders to certain houses. The whole village was filled with sick people wrapped in blankets. Especially children. In fact, you yourself were in a terrible state, Javed. We thought that we were going to lose you. It was when we had lost all hope that this man arrived.

It took him about four days to complete the first round of visits. Until then, he lived on just wheat gruel, the only thing we had to offer him. He spent the nights in an empty corner in our house. We bonded over the songs that I sang in the nights to distract ourselves from the biting cold engulfing us.

His medicines worked well for the entire village. People started recovering one by one. In fact, within two weeks of Dr Anand Shivpuri's arrival, everyone in the village was back on their feet. All of them came to see him and tried to hand over money and their possessions as gifts. But he accepted nothing. 'This was an assignment given by God. He will reward me.'

When he was leaving, the entire village gathered on the banks of the Jhelum to see him off to his own land, Jammu. There was just one thing that the people asked of him as he boarded the shikara – that he come back and set up a hospital for the poor, and live here, among them.

Doctor ji acknowledged their love. And that's how he landed up here in our village, after giving up his home in the city. Our friendship goes back a long, long time.

5

THE STORY THAT JAVED CONTINUED TO TELL

Doctor ji loved music. He could listen to music endlessly. Baba used to go over to Doctor ji's house very often, to sing for the Shivpuri family.

At least once a week, Doctor ji would visit us. And that was to listen to Baba sing.

He set up a small hospital in our village. He never charged anyone exorbitantly. He distributed as many medicines as he could free of cost. He came from an aristocratic family. He built a nice house in the village. He also bought several farmlands and began to cultivate saffron, the wealth of Kashmir. He became a very rich man. But he never distanced himself from the villagers and the village life. Anyone could walk into Dr Anand Shivpuri's house at any time. He was not just my guru, he was the guru of the entire village. We liked him, we loved him, we worshipped him.

But how quickly time changed everything, how quickly things turned. It was then that I realized how much poison religion could inject into the human mind. The fact that he was a Kashmiri Pandit became the only reason why he was soon hated by all the villagers.

During that time, shocking news came in almost every day from Srinagar, Baramulla and Pulwama. Pandits were being driven away from the Kashmir Valley. Their houses were being looted; they were being tortured, they were being killed.

Even as all this was going on, I found solace in the belief that my village would never change. But soon, I started to realize that slowly, my village, too, was being infected by that virus. Many new faces kept surfacing and working on the minds of the people, trying to influence and control them.

'Beta, this madness is temporary. It will die down quickly. We have sailed through infinitely bigger problems to get this far. I trust my village.' This is how Baba quelled my anxiety. But the new clique in the village shattered Baba's belief and turned against the doctor one day. They alleged that the doctor had amassed wealth by fleecing the villagers. They brainwashed people into believing this. They gave Doctor ji an ultimatum to leave the village. But he did not relent. One day, they attacked his house, surrounding it from all sides. Baba tried to rescue him, but he refused to abandon his own house and leave. 'This village invited me over. I lived serving its people. If you decide to reward me for all this with death, I am willing to accept that.'

My Baba was able to save only Doctor ji's wife and son. From that day onwards, my Baba became the enemy of the villagers. What irked them the most was the fact that Baba helped the police capture the people who killed Doctor ji. People started seeing him as the kafir who betrayed the village. He was threatened numerous times by terrorists. But Baba ignored all that. Finally, what everyone in the family feared most, happened. One day, Baba, who went to the Dal Lake as usual, never came back. We searched for him the whole night in vain. On the third day, we found his body floating in the Dal Lake along with a school of giant danio. Along with Doctor ji's death, my education, which was already under threat, also died. I had no option but to take up a job. But there was no way I could find work in the village. We sold the house for whatever we could get and left the village. We rented a house next to the home of a distant relative who lived in Srinagar. Once the family settled in, I came here, to Nainital. I knew that though most boats were moored in Kashmir, they would be moving in Nainital. I was not wrong. I was able to send my family enough money to ensure that they didn't go hungry.

Doctor ji's family sold their house and their farmlands in our village and went to Jammu. But we still stay in touch with each other. Doctor ji's son, Anoop Shivpuri, was then studying in the seventh grade. Today, he is a third-year medical student at the All India Institute of Medical Sciences. Doctor ji's dream which I could not fulfil will now be fulfilled by him. Our son. Our very own Anoop Shivpuri.

And then Javed softly sang an old Lata ji song:

Kyon mein toofan se daroon
Mera saahil aap hai
Koi toofanon se keh de
Mil gaya saahil mujhe

6

THE STORY THAT MOHAN ROY CONTINUED TO TELL

We were in Nainital for only another year or two. Smitha was transferred. And I was tired of that place. Once, when we were all set to travel to Delhi, Javed, after a really long time, dropped in to see us. He came with a small parcel.

'Mohan Saab, since you are going to Delhi, please take a bit of time out for me and go to AIIMS. These are some sweets – please hand this over to our Anoop. Right since childhood, he was very fond of sweets. He will be very happy if you tell him that I sent it for him. It's been a long time since I saw him. I would really like to. When you come back, could you bring me a photograph of his?'

'Yes,' I agreed.

But it turned out to be a bad time to be in Delhi. All the educational institutions were agitating over the Mandal Commission issue. Students from the higher castes and those who were goading them from behind had taken over the city. There were strikes and violence and arson everywhere. It was scary to even step out. Yet, one day, for Javed's sake, we managed to go to AIIMS to hand over the sweets that he had so lovingly sent across for Anoop Shivpuri, the final-year medical student.

But I had to face a very suspicious situation in the hostel. Everyone knew Anoop Shivpuri. He was well known in the college. He was a brilliant student. To many students, he was a hero. But everyone shied away from answering where he was right then. It appeared as though nobody knew anything about his current whereabouts. It was after meeting several students that one of them opened up in strict confidence and told us that Anoop, who was at the forefront of the Mandal agitation, had set himself on fire in public one day and was in hospital in a critical condition with third-degree burns. We went to the hospital, but they were not allowing visitors. He was under police custody. But we met a few of his friends there. We told them that he mattered a great deal to us, handed over our contact numbers, and left after getting them to promise that they would keep us informed.

7

THE AUTHOR'S STORY

Life has a way of settling into a routine, which, in no time, effortlessly sweeps away friends, edging you into a personal pit, making you abandon everyone who anchored you and gave you a sense of rootedness until then.

By the time the story reached where it did, the cable work was complete and the power was restored. Mohan Roy rose all of a sudden. 'Oh God! Finally, it has come! How much time it took! The kids have a class test tomorrow. I'd stepped out a while ago after lighting a candle for them. Wonder if they studied anything. Che! Your department … they have no idea about the value of time.'

In his haste, he had already reached the road. I was trying to ask Mr Mohan Roy to sit for a little while more and complete the story. Did Anoop survive? Did you go to meet him? Did he come to meet you? Did you give Javed's sweets to him? Did you meet Javed after that? I went after him with a flurry of questions.

'The story – we'll save that for later. The kids have a class test tomorrow.' He walked away.

I stopped dead in my tracks like a genie who had lost its magical powers. This, my friend, is the problem with second-hand stories. At a critical moment, the original owner of the story might vanish without telling the entire story. And then, with no recourse to extending the story or relying on imagination, we will have to abandon it halfway – at times like certain dreams, at times like certain lives, and at times like this story.

Bukkaram's Son

On a cold winter morning twenty-three years ago, the young Bitturam Vittal sat amidst the ruins of the Durga Devi temple in Killari, enveloped in a shroud of memories. Around him were the remnants of buildings covered in grass and thorny bushes. A few stone walls still held their ground despite nature's dance of fury, as if to remind the world that there was once a village here. The wells were half covered. In the distance lay parched farmlands. In the desolate sky above, the fear of that day still hung like a dark cloud across which even a bird dared not fly. As far as the eye could see, there was just a frightening silence.

It was after a long hunt that I finally traced Bitturam. Solapur, Osmanabad, Ausa, Latur … there was no place to which I had not travelled in search of him. It was when I was asking around with a CCTV shot of him that Laxman Gaikwad, the famous writer from Maharashtra, instilled hope in me saying that he would find him for me. Until then, though I had collected every possible bit of information about Bitturam, I had not been able to locate him. 'Oh, Bukkaram's son? I saw him a week ago', 'I saw him having tea at this dhaba two days ago', 'Oh! He was here just a while ago' – Bitturam to me was like the snow leopard that kept vanishing right in front of Peter Matthiessen's eyes. But I did not give up; I pursued him stubbornly. And finally, I caught him – in a tea shop in Talani.

'Laxman ji told me that a journalist would come. You are the one, right? But we can't sit here and talk. Bittu's gang will become suspicious if they see us, and then Bittu will have the same fate as Dada ji's,' whispered Bitturam as he escorted me to that godforsaken land which the villagers feared to tread.

Bittu was nine years old then. Even now, like the glimpses of a vision in a sandstorm, there were vague shreds of memory alive in his mind. That was the day everyone came back to their village in high spirits after celebrating Ganeshotsav. The day they slept like logs, tired after a full day of festivities. But Bittu alone could not sleep that night.

'Right from the time we came back home, the dogs in the village kept howling endlessly as though they had seen something scary. The bats that slept all afternoon hanging from the large tree next to the wheat fields were flying around madly in the dark, black sky. The howling of dogs always scared Bittu – whenever he heard them howl, he would push away his brothers lying next to his mother and sink his head into her bosom. But that day, Bittu relented to the persistent crying of his younger brother. Which is why he was awake when the rest of the village slept. It was at some point during the night, when he heard distant rumblings and screams, that Bittu opened the front door and stepped out without telling anyone. He immediately realized that dust was rising rapidly into the sky. He could not understand what was happening. The dogs had stopped howling and were running pell-mell. Curious to find out what was going on, he stepped out on to the street – and at that very moment, Killari shuddered like a person with an ague. He turned around and saw his mud hut crumble like a termite hill. His mother and his four brothers were buried right in front of his eyes. The houses in the village started to collapse one after another. He ran aimlessly through the tremulous street. He didn't get very far. The road ended in a heap of granite rubble which was once the house of the sarpanch. And then it rained continuously for four days in Killari. In the midst of all this, five to eight children emerged from the ruins of the village and joined Bittu. With nothing to do, they huddled together, waiting for the world to end. They forgot the massive wall of caste which had separated them until then.'

Bitturam Vittal paused the telling of his story – one that he narrated weirdly in the third person, almost scared to use the first-person voice – and seemed to recede into a dark silence that stretched across twenty-three long years. In a short while, he snapped out of it.

'This Bittu who is sitting in front of you and his elder brother are the only ones in our family who survived.

Every festival – not just Ganeshotsav – is a big harvest for us. How can we not do anything when people with pocketsful of money walk around lazily, visiting temples and textile shops? My father and my brother were in "distant lands" that day. For father, "distant lands" meant Osmanabad, Latur, and at most, Solapur. He did not know of a world that existed beyond this. It was on his way back with all the goods that he could get, while he was resting in front of Shailendra Babu's watch shop at the very edge of his village, that the earth chose to put Killari in the mixer-grinder. What happened to father that day was published later in the newspapers. The watch-shop owner Shailendra Babu and my father were very good friends for a long, long time. My father did not want to be known as a thief in his own village. For the same reason, he never robbed anyone in Killari, Talani and Sastur. Shailendra Babu, who was aware of this, used to tease him by calling him an unprofessional thief. He would ask my father if he had mastered the art of opening a lock by just looking at it. He would challenge him by asking, "Do you have the courage to break into my shop and steal a watch, Bukkaram?" Now, that would touch a raw nerve in my father who was proud of his lineage. "Why, do you doubt that I do, Shailendra Babu? After all, I am the son of Nathuram Vittal, the great thief who pickpocketed Pandit Nehru when he came to release our community from the Solapur open jail in 1961. The locks which you can open with your eyes exist only in the stories and epics you read. But I can pick the lock of your watch shop as easily as shelling a peanut. Want to see, Babu?" my father would ask. He would then narrate the heroic tales of the various robberies he had carried out, with a liberal sprinkling of high drama. "You wait and see. I will steal your time one day, after I've broken into all the shops in Latur and Osmanabad." It was just to keep his word to his dear friend Shailendra Babu, who was swallowed by the earth forever as he looked on, that on that terrible day, he took with him a clock that had stopped ticking. That was not stealing. Bittu always felt that it was good that he took the clock with him. The next day onwards, the policemen who supposedly came for rescue work were more interested in recovering gold and jewellery that lay buried than people who might still be alive. They did not leave a trace of Shailendra Babu's time behind.'

At that point, Bitturam received a phone call. Bitturam had a guest. He replied that he would come at once. 'They are friends. We are getting ready to go on a journey together. That's why he called. If you'd been a bit late, we would not have met today either.'

He took out a packet of dried tobacco leaves from his pocket and tapped a generous helping of it on to his palm. He then crushed it with his thumb, deposited it into the crater created by limestone between his lip and his teeth, and continued to speak.

'Father did not want any of his children to become thieves – especially after going through the ordeal of helplessly watching his own father being beaten to death by the villagers. He wanted them to become writers like Laxman ji. Doctors like Bhupen ji. Or policemen like Shatappa. Never thieves like Nathuram. "I will never let them be beaten to death by the villagers" – that was my father's pledge. It was not people from another village who beat Nathuram Vittal to death – it was people from his own village. He was once the hero of the village. The hero who basked in the glory of having pickpocketed Nehru walked the streets for a long time with the swagger of Amitabh Bachchan. He never ceased to be proud of that achievement. But eventually, that became his undoing as well.

'For us, the razor blade is Goddess Lakshmi. We do Ayudha pooja every day by spilling the blood of a hen and praying that we do well in our work that day and that we don't fall into the hands of cruel policemen. And then we depart for different towns in search of food for the day. Each gang is made up of four or five people – especially when it comes to pickpocketing in buses and festival grounds. In crowded areas, we would create a net around our target successfully. One person would push him forward and one person would push him backwards. In the meantime, the third one would deftly cut his pocket with a blade and take his purse, which would then at once be handed over to the fourth one. All this would not take more than thirty seconds. In the midst of it all, if by some misfortune, one of us got caught by the people or the police, the rule was that he would not betray his friends, no matter what. We even have a code language to message each other. Scratching the head is a signal to come over, whereas touching the earlobe is a signal of danger. Right since childhood, we've been trained not to say a single word no matter how badly we're beaten up by the police. This Bittu has seen Badabhai – big brother – and others being held against the wall and beaten by Mamu ji.

'But as Nathuram Vittal grew older, he did not have the strength to withstand the thrashing from the villagers. His tongue, hitherto reserved for bragging, started loosening up. He started revealing the names of his friends. He started confessing to the police about crimes he had committed earlier. He started revealing which village he belonged to. In spite of all this, he refused to stop working and sit at home. "This is my traditional occupation. Our ancestors have practised this proudly for thousands of years." Stating that it is beneath his dignity to live without working, he went in search of festival grounds in other lands. And he started getting caught by the police often. When Nathuram Vittal, who had lost his speed, his dexterity and his resilience, became a burden for the village, he was beaten to death like a dog on the street.

'Grief? For Bittu? For what? Nathuram should not have betrayed anyone. That is against our family dharma. That is deceiving Mathari, our family deity. Nathuram Vittal got the death he deserved. But that incident shook my father up quite a bit – even at that age. He realized with great sorrow that this would be the fate of every thief who lost his integrity. Since he was already a thief and since he did not know any other job, he continued to do what he was doing. But when all the others in the village taught their children to be skilled thieves, he sent us to school and taught us the alphabet. But our Mamu ji lured Badabhai away when he was a kid, with paan, gutkha and small change. In spite of father advising against it, Badabhai gave up school and became a professional thief. In fact, it was because he was with Mamu ji in Solapur or Pune on that fateful day of the Ganesh Festival that he escaped the earthquake. That was the only reason why I am happy he was a thief. If not, Bittu would have lost him too that night.

'Our gold and other belongings were taken away by the police. The clothes you sent with so much love went to the second-hand textile shops in Bombay. The benefits that the government sanctioned for us were siphoned off by the middlemen. Everyone just got a house free. From then on, it was Mamu ji who brought Bittu up. He hated the fact that Bittu was going to school. He kept scolding Bittu, asking him to stop studying and take up his traditional trade. He starved Bittu, hit him, and even kicked him out of the house to achieve this. But Bittu studied hard to fulfil his father's dream. Until he got a degree. It was Badabhai who helped him fund his education. Using money stolen by his brother, Bittu dreamt of a future where he wouldn't have to steal.

'Mamu ji always made fun of Bittu. "Son, there is a big difference between a dream and real life. You will understand that when you grow up. You will then toe my line. Until then, you study." It was only when he set out to find a job with a painstakingly earned Bachelor's degree in Marathi under his belt that he understood what this meant. The British had written us off as the thieving clan. It was the same fate when India took over. We were given a very high-sounding label: de-notified nomadic tribe. We didn't feature anywhere in the endless reservation quotas in the country. Yet, there was not an examination he did not write, not an interview he did not attend. He qualified in many of them. But to get the job, one needed to pay. Lakhs. Five lakhs for a peon. Ten lakhs for a clerk. Amounts that were too big for a brother who was a mere pickpocket to pay. Today, nobody walks around with money in their purse, Saab. They use cards for anything and everything. Now, all we get is the small change you might have in your pocket. The risks in the job have gone up substantially. The streets are lined with policemen. The shops are filled with security personnel. There are CCTV cameras everywhere. Just imagine our miserable life in this new age. It was beyond Badabhai to buy what Bittu dreamed of more than anything else – a decent job.

'Bittu went to Pune. He thought that a job in the city would be easy – like the fat purse in the pocket of a careless, rich man sauntering down the road – something that he could get without too much effort. But that was not the experience that that city gifted him.

'Nobody would give people like Bittu work. We are thieves by birth. You will study the environment during the day and set out to steal at night. "Go, go," they would say, as though chasing stray dogs away. They wouldn't believe that it was not to steal, they wouldn't believe that it was just to try to make a decent living. Until the stamp of caste fades away from our faces, nobody will believe, Saab. Bittu worked as a salesman in a textile shop for two weeks. When the supervisor who was on leave came back, he drove Bittu away, saying, "You reek of your caste. Get lost. Go and wash toilets." Another three years went by searching and begging for jobs. But nobody offered one.

'Bittu came back to Killari. The last resort was to plough the fields in his village. But Bittu was cheated again. It was two years since it had rained. Nobody was farming any more. Crops were leaving the barren fields. Everyone was leaving the village. Vidarbha was slowly crawling towards us.'

The evening was fading into night. We walked back to the gram panchayat where my car was parked. Frail bulls pulling heavy carts laden with goods for distant lands passed by. It was time to part. 'Friends will reach now,' Bitturam said. 'It's Sivaratri the day after tomorrow. Ten lakh devotees will come to Allahabad. This kind of a crowd is a dream come true for a thief. Go, tell the people who have read my father's story that Bukkaram's son continues to live as Bukkaram. And that he has no wonderful, inspiring stories to present to the new age.'

A short while later, an old vehicle drove up. It was so crammed with youngsters that even air would have found it hard to pass through. Yet Bitturam managed to squeeze himself in along with them and closed the door with great difficulty. He left for Allahabad to celebrate Sivaratri. And I went back to the police station in my hometown to write out a report that I was unable to find Bitturam the thief, so that I could close another case file.

Alice in Wonderland

'WAS IT ABOUT THIS CLEAR sea that that idiot wrote "snot green sea, the sea that gets you by the balls, the sea that's as dark as wine"?'

It was not this irritating question, but her fathomless beauty that struck me first. That Brazilian beauty was dipping her legs in the clear Irish waters of Forty Foot, the swimmers' paradise in Sandycove.

'That guy is definitely half gone,' said her friend, who, too, was gently splashing the water with her legs.

Though I hung around on the pretext of taking selfies, my male eyes could not help but keep returning to that samba beauty. That was when she said this. I decided to make this the sea bridge that would lead me to her. I said with great passion, 'The sea! The sea! The man that you all condemn has also written that the sea is our great, beloved mother!'

'Oh! A great Joyce fan, are you? There, go to that museum, take a couple of pictures and put them on Facebook. You'll get all the likes you want,' she said unkindly and went back to teasing the water with her feet.

The next day, as I raised my eyes after placing a rose at the eternal resting place of Yeats at the Drumcliffe Church at the foot of the Ben Bulben valley, I found myself looking straight into her face. For a moment, I was dazed. Like the disquieting flutter of a bat's wings, the face that had kept me awake all of last night was right in front of me again. The face that I thought would have by now become one with the zillion faces of another city, never to be seen again. Though quite taken aback, and having wilted a bit at the ruthless onslaught yesterday, my face remained devoid of any expression. But without any hesitation, she gave me a warm smile.

'What a coincidence!' I muttered, as though I had entered a magical world. 'This is no coincidence! All the vehicles of the tour companies travel the same beaten track. Don't be surprised if we meet again for a third time somewhere tomorrow,' she said lightly. 'So, like me, you're on a literary trail, aren't you?' I took a few steps forward on the bridge that I had tried to build yesterday. 'It's easy to figure out that she who knows her Joyce is not into pulp literature. The Irish Revolution and Its Literature are what I am researching at the University of São Paulo. I won a scholarship. Why give up a free trip? So I just boarded a flight and came down.' She answered many of the questions that I was planning to ask. 'So, who was the writer that captured the quintessence of the Irish mind?

James Joyce? Yeats? Shaw? Or Oscar Wilde?' I walked out of the cemetery with her, determined to make the most of this new bridge. 'What's the big doubt? It's the man who wrote "Being Irish, he had an abiding sense of tragedy, which sustained him through temporary periods of joy" – yes, it's Yeats. No other writer understood this land as well as he did. But the idiots in this country have placed the other donkey on a pedestal.' She took her friend's hand in hers and walked towards the car. The friend still wore the same sardonic look as she did yesterday, without even the slightest change.

'So, we might meet again tomorrow, right?' I walked up behind her and asked.

'Yes. At the Giant's Garden from Oscar Wilde's story. At four in the evening,' she said, as she got into the car.

'I forgot to ask you one thing … your name.'

'What's in a name? *Cast a cold eye, on life, on death. Horseman, pass by!*'

Her car, a chariot of joy, abandoned me in front of the church and the cemetery, and vanished into the horizon. She was evolving into a mysterious puzzle.

I turned up early at the Giant's Garden in Merrion Square Park for the third meeting at three o'clock. But how on earth would I find her in this garden that spanned acres? Amidst thousands of visitors who were walking around, amidst the crowd that thronged the endless pathway lined with Christmas trees, among the couples resting on the vast green lawns – where would I find her? The needle on the watch moved on from four to four-thirty and then five. My legs were aching from all the walking. 'Come, let's go. She would have taken some other route,' my fellow-traveller said irritably. 'Let's walk one more round, and then we'll leave,' I said, pacifying him. As we walked the last round, I saw her on a swing, in the children's park. As soon as she saw me in the distance, she got off the swing and came running.

'An Indian who lives up to his thousand-year legacy – never on time,' she chided. I told her the story of how I had reached at three and how, all this while, I had been walking around the park looking for her. 'The idiot who loves James Joyce, no doubt. When you say Oscar Wilde, where else should one search other than in the children's park?'

To hide my embarrassment, I came up with another question and asked her how she had figured out my Indian legacy.

She retorted, 'You can be sure that when a man meets a woman, if he looks into her eyes first, he is a human being, and if he looks at her breasts first, he is an Indian.' Upon hearing this, her friend burst out laughing.

'Alice, you are a bad girl. Did you see how his face drooped?' she said as she laughed.

Alice! I savoured the name as I whispered it to myself. Alice! I looked into your eyes first, not your breasts; at the brilliance of your beauty. *All changed, changed utterly: A terrible beauty is born!*

'Come, let's go. There's something about her that's not right,' my fellow-traveller whispered in my ear.

'Wait, we can't just leave like that. We wandered around so much. Let's have a beer at the Oscar Bar before we leave. But you will have to pay our bill too,' she insisted, as though she understood what my fellow-traveller had whispered to me. We had no option but to agree.

'A bar in the name of a poet. And a people who are proud of that. In spite of being reputed drunkards, we never could open a John Abraham Bar or an Ayyappan Toddy Shop or a Punathil Pub,' said my fellow-traveller as we crossed the road.

Sitting in the dimly lit bar, on either side of a table with the cold spirits, the four of us spoke about literature for a long time. Most of the time, we were debating Joyce. In between, her friend kept reminding her, 'It's time to go.'

'We've taken up a part-time night job,' said Alice, explaining why her friend was in a hurry.

'Even as a tourist?' I exclaimed, my face lighting up with amazement.

'Of course! Only arrogant, proud folks will spend the weak currency from our third-world countries in Europe. The money that we want to spend here, we'll earn from here. And if there's anything left over, we'll take it back home with us.'

'Great!' I stood up and shook her hand. It was genuine appreciation. 'If the idea is to hold my hand, go right ahead. But there will be a fee for every minute,' she said, putting me off.

After another round of drinks, as we were leaving, I took out my phone for a selfie. But she refused.

'They call this morphing phobia in my country,' I teased her. She laughed.

'This is not the fear of the internet. Our belief does not allow us to share our photographs with anyone,' she explained.

'Belief?' I raised my eyebrows.

'Yes, she follows Umbanda – and those who follow Umbanda don't give their photographs to strangers,' her friend explained.

'Why?'

'I will tell you about all that later. Now it's time to report for work.' Both of them got up.

'When do we meet next?' I asked.

'We'll meet at a pub during the weekend. Give me your phone number, I'll call.' She took my fellow-traveller's number and walked away.

Her name. Her radiant face. Frothing beer. These were etched in my mind. The only thing I did not comprehend was the religion called Umbanda. This became my obsession during all the time I had to myself that whole week. I searched for Umbanda on the internet. There were several videos, pictures and a lot of information available. It seemed to be a mélange of African traditions, Roman Catholicism, Spiritism and ancient American beliefs. When I shared my findings with my fellow-traveller, he warned me, 'Be careful. She could be a black-magic woman. She will not hesitate to do what she pleases.' But like desire that cannot be chained, I eagerly waited for her call.

That weekend, at exactly nine in the evening, the call landed on my fellow-traveller's phone. 'Come to The Temple Bar. We'll meet before the wine glass of James Joyce.'

The Temple Bar, the famous pub in Dublin, was a thirty-minute walk from our hotel. It was drizzling. We braved the bite of the cold wind and set off. People were flowing in and out of the pub. Single mynahs and pigeon-couples were swaying to the music and the wine, revelling in the magic of the night. We navigated our way through the crowd and then a maze of rooms, and just as we reached the statue of James Joyce drinking wine and reading *The Dubliner*, her call came. 'Why don't you say cheers to that imbecile? Don't you need a photograph to post on Facebook tomorrow, worshipper?'

'Alice! Where are you?'

'I'm in a bit of a hurry. If you really want to see me, wait. I'll get there.' She hung up. Her words, 'If you really want to see me', contained deep within, like a nano chip, the energy that I needed to wait for her that whole night. I waited. Downing beer, enjoying the music, watching people around me. I rejected my fellow-traveller's invitation to wander around a bit and come back to the Temple Bar. I was afraid that I would miss seeing her. 'What work could she be doing this late in the night?' I asked my fellow-traveller.

'Waitressing in a bar, what else?' Having waited this long, the exasperation was very evident in his voice. The clock in the Dublin Fort turned three or four full circles. Tired of celebrating, people were easing themselves slowly out of the pub. 'She will not turn up,' my travel companion said furiously at regular intervals. I countered by saying that my plan was to wait until she turned up. I never got up from there other than a couple of times when travellers wanted to take photographs by Joyce's statue. My travel companion was convinced that I had lost it.

But my wait and her promise were not in vain. Turn up she did. That, too, in a great hurry, without even having removed the make-up that she seemed to have worn to work.

'You need to learn to keep a promise. How you teased us last week – Indians – the tradition of a thousand years. What now?' My fellow-traveller took out his frustration on her.

'Did I ask you to wait?' she asked, looking at me seated in the empty pub.

'I wanted to see you,' I said.

'Writers are like fishermen who put out their bait and wait. Until the story bites, he will wait in any pub, wait as long as it takes, right?'

'No, Alice, I just wanted to see you. Shall I order beer?'

'I'm really tired. Let's meet some other day.'

'I will not be here until the next weekend.'

'We'll meet before that. Alice means noble. And that will reflect in my action.'

Before leaving, she opened her bag and handed over a bottle of herbal medicine. 'This medicine was prepared and blessed by the guru of the Umbandas, Macumbara, the ingredients of which were sourced from the Amazon forests. If you bathe in water laced with this concoction for seven days, whatever you desire will be yours. That's for sure. This is my gift to you for having waited this long for me tonight.'

'Accept it. It's from the Amazon forest, right? Even if your desires don't come true, it might do your sores and itches some good,' my fellow-traveller said sarcastically.

'Hey, mister. You should give me a photograph of yours. I'll show you what will come your way – a sore, or leprosy.' Alice turned on my travel companion.

'Don't give your photograph, my friend. She will get Macumbara to do black magic. Your entire family will perish,' Alice's friend said, fear audible in her voice.

That night ended thus.

The next day, she called me on my travel companion's mobile. 'Sorry, Indians. I tried my level best to excuse myself early from work yesterday. The weekend boom was on. And those rogues said that I could not leave.'

'It's just a part-time job. You walk out and find the next one,' my experience said.

'I just said part-time the other day. We've actually come here on a three-month contract.'

'As a bar waitress?'

'No. Night. Bar. Contract. You can guess what it is, right?'

'No. Make it clear.'

'You come to my pub one day. I'll tell you.'

I took down her address and hung up. I could make out certain things. For the same reason, I did not want to share all that she had said with my travel companion.

The next evening, I stepped out into the city alone. There were two giant bouncers in front of the pub she worked in. They did not let me get in even though I made it clear that I was there because Alice had invited me. After quibbling for a while, I finally had to pay the entry fee of fifteen euros to get in. Unlike other pubs, it was darkness and silence that greeted me here. There were only about ten or fifteen people around the bar counter. They sat with their heads hung as though the silence they swallowed had done them in.

Suddenly, I heard a female voice from a dark corner of the pub. A group of half-naked women stepped into the light. Alice was one of them. She came over and gave me a hug. Her beauty lit up my face and caused a flutter in my heart. I tried to move away gently. But she continued to hold me close for a while. Alice then introduced me to the other women. One of them opened a packet of cigarettes and asked me for an autograph. Her friends laughed out loud. Alice shooed them away and then whispered in my ear, 'Come, let's go down.' I followed her like a faithful dog. 'Fifty euros,' growled the man behind the counter. Alice took the money out of my pocket and gave it to him. 'No touching the body. You can only enjoy the dance,' the man growled again and closed the door.

The floor below was bathed in a blue light. Here, Alice took off her clothes one by one and danced the dance of an enchantress – a performance that lasted about ten minutes. She then sat beside me and touched me. I was like a shirt that had been ironed with a cold iron.

O vanity of Sleep, Hope, Dream, endless Desire,
The Horses of Disaster plunge in the heavy clay:
Beloved, let your eyes half close, and your heart beat
Over my heart, and your hair fall over my breast…

She leaned on my shoulder. Her fragrance seeped into me. 'You must be on fire like a man. The intoxication of that fire must bring you here again. That is what I desire. If you don't, they will see it as my professional failure,' she said into my ear.

'Yes. I will come again. To see you. But I want you to tell me how you landed up in this.'

'I'll call you tomorrow.'

I thought she would never call me again. But she called again the next day. I knew why:

'My papa was the Macumbara of a small coastal village near São Paulo, who took care of the needs of the fisherfolk, all Umbanda followers. He was a rustic soul who wanted his children to have a good education. I was the smartest of his children. After school, I wanted to study in one of the good universities in São Paulo. It was then that a man from the city, who came in search of Macumbara, offered to help us. He promised Papa that if I go to São Paulo, he would get me admission at a good university. So, my papa and I went to São Paulo. It was a trap. We realized that he was part of a drug and trafficking cartel. He ordered Papa to leave me there and go back to the village. They started quarrelling. He cold-bloodedly shot my papa right in front of my eyes. My father cursed him before dying: "May your daughter live through everything that you make my daughter live through." I was taken by the gang. To this day, I haven't been able to free myself from their clutches.'

'Alice … if what you are saying is true, you have so many ways to escape. Now you are in a foreign country.'

'It's just an illusion. I am like a puppy dog that's been let out of its kennel. My owners' eyes are on me all the time. My friend whom you saw with me is part of their gang.'

'What can I do for you?'

'Don't think of doing anything that is not required. Don't try to act brave; look at what happened to my papa. Pretend that we never met. I don't want any trace left of the fact that a person like me existed, not even in someone's mind. In fact, I did not want you to take my photograph because of this.'

'I would like to see you once more before I leave.'

'Come to my pub. We'll meet. But only as a customer. No sympathy there.'

I hung up. No; she hung up after leaving me in a state. Who is she to you? How does it matter who she is? There are so many women in the world like her. What is so special about her? She goes her way, and you go yours. My mind was in turmoil the whole night – there was no resolution I could come up with even by morning. So, I posted on Facebook: 'If any of my two thousand friends have any connection in the Irish Secret Service, please call. I need their help.' Half an hour later, a friend called and said his neighbour was a very senior official in the Gardaí. I gave him an idea of the situation Alice was in. He said he would soon call me back. It was the senior official in the Gardaí who called. He probed in detail and collected all the information from me. I gave him Alice's number to make things easy. I felt very proud that I could come to the rescue of a woman trapped in a foreign land. Alice, it was perhaps for this that we met at Forty Foot – for the next turning point in your life. Now you will never be able to say that Indians gaze at a woman's breasts first. You will have to say that they look into your heart. For sure.

How many loved your moments of glad grace,
And loved your beauty with love false or true,
But one man loved the pilgrim soul in you,
And loved the sorrows of your changing face…

Exactly two hours later, the officer called me. I answered with great joy and hope. 'You idiot! How dare you waste our time by telling us nonsense about respectable women! I could have asked that woman to give me a written complaint and arrested you. Because she was a good soul, she did not agree.' Before I could ask him anything, he hung up in a huff.

After hearing the story, my travel companion burst out laughing, saying, 'You deserve this.' It was then that she called. 'You've proven again that you are a total Joyce devotee. I told you that you should not attempt to do anything brave. What came of it? Wasted time and effort – and abuse to boot. Right?' she teased.

'Alice, this was an opportunity. But you did not make use of it. Which means that you enjoy this life of yours, right?'

'Yes.'

'Meaning…'

'I cooked up that story. I just wanted to work you up. Truth be told, my story is a different one. A happy one.'

'A different one?'

'Yes. Remember, I told you about a mafia king in the last story? A creep who goes to villages to hunt for girls and lure them in? The man who cold-bloodedly shot Macumbara? He is my papa. The man who rakes in money by selling drugs and women sent his daughter on a holiday to Europe. This comfortable life of mine is built on the tears of many, many innocent girls. Can someone who has studied literature enjoy this kind of a life? Or sleep peacefully? This is the only way I can take revenge on him. What he forces girls from across the world to do, I do here of my own free will. Anyway, Macumbara's curse is still alive. How can I escape that? I have no regret, no tears about what I do. Only great joy.'

Disbelief caught my tongue for a while. 'Three stories. Which one is true?' I asked.

'Which is the one that you like best?' she asked.

I did not say anything.

'No matter which story I say is true, you will still believe only the version that you choose to. It applies not just to stories – life, too, has this limitation.'

'One more thing. Is your name really Alice?'

She laughed out loud.

'What's in a name, Indian? *Cast a cold eye, on life, on death. Horseman, pass by!*'

Addis Ababa

WHO ON EARTH WOULD GIVE up a military-quota bottle – be it back home in Kerala or in the Gulf? It was during one of my many attempts to lay my hands on this liquid gold that I met Kevin Peter.

There's an American naval base out here, where I work. One of my friends had told me that all I had to do was befriend an officer here to get premium stuff for a song. And one fine day, I was presented with the perfect opportunity to do just that. The company that I worked for had recently bagged a contract to supply furniture to the American naval base – and yours only was in charge of delivery. My liquor route suddenly looked navigable.

But after two or three trips to the naval base, I realized that it wouldn't be smooth sailing. I tried befriending the whites in more ways than one during the small breaks that I had between fitting and placing furniture. But none of them showed any signs of warming up to TCN.

After landing here, for a few years, I thought people called me TCN because it was the abbreviation for Thomas

Chandy Neduveliparambil. In those days, I was very proud of being thus addressed. Thomas Chandy sounded ordinary. TCN sounded quite stylish. It was with such effortlessness that the Americans gave gravitas to my name. I even started introducing myself thus: 'I'm TCN.' But soon, I smelled a rat when I realized that they were calling every passing Bengali and Pakistani 'TCN' – they couldn't all be Thomas Chandy Neduveliparambils, could they? When I realized later that this was an abbreviation for 'Third Country National', a nickname for everyone from that part of the world, the TCN in me died a thousand deaths. Yet, drowning in the temptation of premium liquor at a non-premium price, I stated my desire in broken, staccato English to a few people at the base – all of them seemed outraged at my audacity and just shook their heads as if to say that it was all illegal. Every time, I would feel small and disappointed – especially because a few of my friends with glib tongues were often rewarded with the nectar. I stopped asking.

But Kevin Peter was different. From the day we met, he behaved affably, without the usual scorn that was reserved for TCNs. As luck would have it, my company received a big order from Kevin's department. It took us about a month to deliver and set up that lot of furniture, which was imported from Malaysia. Considering the fact that we had been meeting every day for this long, I managed to work up the courage to ask Kevin for a bottle.

Kevin shrugged his shoulders in helplessness. 'My quota for this month is over. We'll see next month.' He took down my number. One week into the next month, I completed the assignment and left that site. Kevin did not call me until then. And when I did meet him a couple of times, the Thomas Chandy Neduveliparambil in me prevented me from asking him about this again.

It was when I had reconciled myself to the fact that nothing was going to happen that I received a call. The pure American accent made me stammer. I asked the guy on the other end of the line to call the company directly if it was anything related to furniture. He managed to tell me in slow English that it was Kevin Peter who was calling and that it was to give me the bottle that I had once asked for.

'Where should I come?' I asked.

'Come to my apartment in the evening.'

Kevin gave me his home address.

It was not just the thought of premium liquor that made me really high that whole day. It was also the fact that to my friends, I would now be an influential guy who could source a bottle directly from an American.

That evening, I got out a bit early from work, armed with the address that Kevin had given me. It did not take much effort to find the posh apartment complex where the well-heeled stayed. A TCN there elicited many questions and a physical inspection. Finally, the Punjabi security personnel let me in very reluctantly. I got into the elevator that had mirrors on all three sides, got out on the fifth floor, walked along the granite corridor, reached apartment number fifty-four, and rang the bell. For a while, there was no response. Was Kevin not here? If I had known his number, I could have called him. As I stood there deciding what to do next, the door opened. It was a black girl with a long nose, pouty lips, and hair that appeared as though tails of a hundred rats were hanging from her head. She was wearing jeans and a T-shirt that revealed the outline of a well-endowed body. I got a bit flustered because I was not expecting someone like this in Kevin's apartment. I asked for Kevin.

'He's not back from work yet. What is it?' she asked lazily, chewing gum.

I stuttered and stammered and told her the story of the bottle.

She abandoned me at the door and went inside. I heard her talk to someone on the phone. She came back and invited me in.

Good Lord! I, Thomas Chandy Neduveliparambil, alone in an apartment with a black American woman! I summoned up a bit of courage and stepped in. I sat on the edge of the feather-soft sofa.

'Tea?' she asked, without any formality.

'No, thanks.' That was the Malayali in me, programmed to say 'no' to everything first.

'Well, I need a cup of tea. I'm going to make tea.' She walked into the kitchen.

'Then I will also have a cup,' I said a bit loudly. There was a secret behind why I had the courage to speak a tad loudly. I was shrewd enough to make out in the short exchange we had that her English was no better than mine. Which meant this blackie was also an immigrant. I knew that black-American English often left a lot to be desired.

Two thoughts crossed my mind before she came into the room again with the tea. First, the irony of me, someone who would never ever be acknowledged as a 'white' guy even in his own home state of Kerala, labelling an American as a blackie. And second, the largeheartedness of Kevin: I've always respected the American mind that accepts mates without colour discrimination. I've always looked on in wonder when a white man and a black woman or a black man and a white woman walk down the street, hand in hand. This was not surprising considering the fact that I was the person who, in the arrogance of having made a bit of money after locating to the Middle East, wrote to his dad that even if my prospective bride is not all that well-educated, she should be fair, like the Malayali actress Lissy. Was she Kevin Peter's wife or his girlfriend? Whoever she was, it was admirable. My respect as well as my sympathy for Kevin Peter went up considerably in that short period of time.

She placed a steaming cup of tea on the teapoy, sat on the sofa opposite mine and blew gently into the hot tea before taking a sip. She then asked me a set of standard questions. Are you working with Kevin? How long is it since you came here? What's your nationality? Where's your family? How many kids? When are you going back home for the holidays?

I replied in detail to every question. I decided that I, too, should ask her something. So, after giving it a bit of thought, I asked her what her name was.

'Rose Williams.'

'You would be Venus Williams'…?' This comic, 'Innocent-style' question tickled her quite a bit. She laughed out loud revealing her white teeth. Another lighthearted comment came to mind: The courage your father had in calling a blackie like you 'Rose' is admirable. But I did not say it. She asked me my name.

'I am Mr TCN.'

'What?' she asked, leaning forward, curious.

I expanded TCN, lest she found the abbreviation offensive. 'Thomas Chandy Neduveliparambil.' She burst out laughing. So did I. She was about to say something. But at that point, Kevin opened the door and came in. I jumped up. Kevin shook my hand and apologized for being late. He thanked Rose for serving tea and gave her a kiss. He then handed over the bottle he had brought with him. I offered him the money for the same. He declined and said it was a gift. Overjoyed, I put the money back into my pocket. Kevin asked me not to tell anyone about the bottle and to call once in a while if I needed more. Just as I was about to leave, he asked me if I could get him a small teapoy for the ashtray. After accepting a bottle free, how could I refuse? I promised him that I would. Kevin described the teapoy that he had in mind. I placed my hand on my heart – to create something like that would cost three times the amount of money that I had just put back into my pocket. But I kind of appreciated what Kevin and Rose had done for me. It was with a bit of pride that I stepped into the elevator of the apartment complex – proud that I was man enough to establish friendship with an American.

I went back to hand over the teapoy that Kevin Peter had asked for, and then again to accept another bottle in return. Both times, Rose Williams welcomed me happily. But the third time I went there, as I reached the front door, I heard a woman screaming loudly inside. And then the sound of things falling and breaking. I could indistinctly hear two people yelling at each other. Yes, it was Kevin and Rose. I suddenly had a very base curiosity to know why they were fighting. But the Thomas Chandy Neduveliparambil in me did now allow me to stand there and eavesdrop. I was about to ring the bell, when I decided against it and walked away. I did not want to meet them when they were in this state. It was not just the thought of hurting them, it was also because I was hurt. I was sad that I had to listen to the dark moments of my ideal black-and-white couple. Anyway, these people are like this. They will live together for a while and then part. I comforted myself thinking this is all very common for them. After that, for some reason, my relationship with Kevin broke off.

This was because the business orders my company got from them dwindled, and a couple of times, when I asked for a bottle, in return, Kevin demanded furniture that was way too expensive.

Much later, very unexpectedly, I met Rose Williams again at a ladies' bar, where she was working as a waitress! I was dumbfounded. An American lady. The wife or girlfriend of somebody in a high position in the military like Kevin Peter. And she works as a waitress in a bar where third world people like me drink. I did not make an attempt to catch her attention. I also thought that it would be highly unlikely that she would remember me. But to my utter surprise, as soon as she saw me, she approached my table and said, 'Hi, Mr TCN.'

'You? Here?'

'Why? You don't like a girl like me working and making some money?' she retorted.

'No, not that. An American like you in a TCN bar...'

She laughed out loud.

'So that's the reason. Who told you that I am an American? I am also a poor TCN without a green card. In Kevin's words, an African nigger. Rather than go to fancy bars and serve white pigs like him, I'd rather serve ordinary people like you. The tips here would be much less. But I'm fine with that.'

She placed the menu on my table and moved on to the next. I sat there not knowing what to think or say.

'How come I don't see you there any more?' she asked when she came to take the order. 'Did you stop your bottle business with Kevin?'

'That business was a loss for me,' I said.

'Don't you know that a Yankee will never stay on in a business which will result in a loss for him?' She laughed as though she were teasing me.

'Do you still live with Kevin?' I asked bravely, putting together that incident at the flat and her current demeanour.

'Of course! He's my husband. We still love each other and live together under the same roof,' she said.

That confused me again. God! I just didn't understand this African woman. Did she hate or love Kevin Peter? I ordered two beers and a beef fry.

We did not talk much more that day. As I was leaving, she took my phone number. She asked me to drop in sometime and said that she would call. The usual promotional lines that bar girls use, I thought. But she walked with me to the entrance, and there, slipped the bill and the tip that I had kept for her back into my pocket, and whispered into my ear, 'This African nigger does not need your measly tip to get by.'

What a strange creature, I thought.

Though I did not frequent ladies' bars, I went there a couple of times after that to see Rose Williams. I was interested to know more about her.

'I would like to know more about you,' I told her bluntly one day.

'What's there to know about me? You're a TCN. And I'm a TCN. To everyone, I am an African nigger, a blackie. There's nothing more than that.'

She moved away. When I realized that she would not open up, I slowly stopped going to the bar. Suddenly one day, she called.

'Hello, Mr TCN,' she teased. By then, I had an aversion to being addressed like that. So much so that I did not even say hello. She sensed that I was sulking.

'Oh! You're sulking? That, too, because I called you TCN just to tease you? Then I'll have to fall out with the whole world – I hear African bitch, nigger, blackie and what have you, on a daily basis.'

'All this comes from your inferiority complex. The days of discrimination on the basis of colour are long gone,' I quipped, not to be outdone.

'Really? Think again. When you saw me first, did you not think "negro" or "blackie" first?'

That hit me hard. I apologized.

'You don't have to say you're sorry. That's what the world is used to doing,' she comforted me. 'By the way, I did not call you now to bleat about colour discrimination. You've been aching to know about me for a long time, right? Come to my apartment on the twenty-first of this month, at nine in the evening. I will show you a sight that will blow your mind.'

'What are you going to show me?'

'Don't be so impatient, TCN. Come and take a look.' She hung up abruptly, leaving me with my questions unasked.

The twenty-first was a while away. In the hope that I might be able to meet her once again before that, I visited the bar. But her friends told me that it had been a few days since she turned up for work.

I tried calling her in between. 'I'm busy, TCN. Do come on the twenty-first,' she said and hung up.

Should I go to an African woman's house all by myself – that, too, in the night? After much debate, I decided to accept her invitation. I was really curious about the mind-blowing sight she had in store for me.

Just as she had instructed, I was at the door to her apartment at nine. The sardar ji security guard smiled in recognition and asked, 'Is there a party happening there today? Quite a few guests have gone up.' Though I had no idea, I nodded in the affirmative. While I was in the elevator, I thought that it might probably be her birthday today. Even though she did not say it, I should have guessed. Oops! I should have bought a gift. It would be so embarrassing to walk in empty-handed. I went down in the elevator just as I had gone up. I bought a small gift from a nearby store, had it wrapped in coloured paper and came back.

I could hear music and voices even as I walked towards the apartment. It was good that I had bought the gift –

if I hadn't, it would have been really embarrassing, the TCN in me was certain. I rang the bell and waited. The door was opened by a black giant. His stare asked me what I wanted. I stammered. I tried to peer into the apartment to see if Kevin or Rose were in sight. But they were not. The room was full of black men and women. They were all probably people from Rose's Africa. I was a bit worried if I would fit in their midst. And then, as luck would have it, a girl who had seen me in the bar a couple of times walked up to the door. They spoke to each other in their language. Yet, it was a bit reluctantly that the black giant let me in.

I asked the girl about Rose. Without saying anything, she pointed to a room inside. I could hear singing and the sound of drums come from the room. That room, too, was full of black men and women. I could not see what was happening inside. I tried worming my way through the crowd to see if I could spot Rose or Kevin, but one of them stopped me and made me stand at the fag end of a queue. It was then that I understood that there was a queue. As I inched my way into the room, I realized that what Rose had said was true. It was indeed a mind-boggling sight. Rose was seated on a large chair that resembled a throne. She was wearing a crown and a large collection of African bead chains around her neck. She was dressed in an antique costume. A line of men and women sat in front of her, singing, playing a percussion instrument which sounded like the maddalam. As the people in the queue passed her by, they kissed her hand and placed their gifts at her feet. She kept raising her hand as though to bless each one of them.

Truth be told, I was a bit scared. It appeared as though she were the personification of a goddess of some ancient African religion, who was conducting a mysterious ritual. I looked around for Kevin in an attempt to connect with something familiar. God! Did these people sacrifice him, or eat him? Did they invite me to make me a sacrificial lamb? Fear made me want to pee. In fact, I peed two drops. I wanted to run out. But there were black guys all around me. There was no way I could escape them. I was certain that they would finish me off.

Rose smiled when she saw me. She waved her hand. She must have read my pale face. She said something to her friends who were nearby. They looked at me and burst out laughing. After standing in the queue like a cat that had fallen into hot water, I finally managed to get to where she was sitting and offered her my gift. She blessed me. I bent down and greeted her like everyone else before me had done. Her friends got me a chair to sit on in one corner of the room. I was aching to leave. But I sat down. The first group of people finished singing and moved away. The next group came forward. They swung their legs from left to right, swayed rhythmically to the percussion, and started singing in a language that I could make neither head nor tail of. But it sounded really good. I sat and enjoyed the music halfheartedly. In the meantime, a few black men came over, said hello, and shook my hand. I was getting increasingly worried about when the sacrifice would happen.

Thankfully, there was no sacrifice that night. The song and dance went on until midnight. And then there was a great feast. By two o'clock, everyone kissed each other goodbye. I, too, was able to leave only then. Rose accompanied me to the door.

'Were you scared?' she asked, laughing. 'I'll call and tell you everything in detail,' she reassured me.

I was really not interested in hearing or knowing anything more. Black-magic woman, nigger, blackie. Yet, after a week, when she invited me over to her apartment, I accepted: there was no killing the innate curiosity of TCN.

It was Rose who opened the door when I rang the bell. She was wearing her usual jeans and T-shirt. She had changed her hairstyle a bit. I glanced inside. Thankfully there were no other blacks there.

'No song and dance today?' I asked, largely to assuage the tension that was building up in my mind.

'Looks like you liked the programme…'

'Of course. People like to see scenes that terrify them a second time.'

'I just wanted to shock you. And you got scared. That's good.'

'Where's Kevin?' I asked.

'Why? Are you scared, TCN, to spend a bit of time with a black woman in this apartment, without Kevin? I'll make some tea.'

She walked off to the kitchen but came back with a tray laden with a premium bottle, two glasses, two sodas, an ice box and a bowl of nuts.

'I have served you many times before. Today, let's sit together and drink. What say?'

'Sure. But you have to stop alluding to yourself as a nigger,' I said.

'I am not ashamed of it in any way. Not only that, I am also proud of who I am.'

I did not pursue the matter. She poured two drinks. We picked it up, said cheers and took a sip each. We did not speak until we had finished the first drink. She then poured a second round of drinks. We sat and polished that off too.

'Rose, tell me, what happened here that day?' The Thomas Chandy Neduveliparambil in me woke up. She laughed.

'What do you think happened here that day?' she asked as soon as she had stopped laughing.

'It was either a mysterious religious prayer or a birthday celebration unique to your land. And if not that, the total madness of negroes!'

She laughed again and said, 'All your assumptions are totally wrong. I'll tell you.' She poured another drink for both of us. After a brief interval, during which we quietly sipped our drinks, she said, 'My name is not Rose Williams. Like many of the temporary things in my life, that name too is temporary. I'm Eleni Hadiya Sassy.

From the small town of Hosaena, on the banks of the river Gihon, in the tenth province of Ethiopia. Though Ethiopia was the land of poverty and deserts, my Hosaena was rich and prosperous, with grasslands, cattle, and coffee plantations. My family had coffee plantations that you would not be able to cover even if you drove for one whole day in a vehicle; cattle that you would not be able to take stock of even if you counted for an entire year; forty thousand servants, and six mansions – even today I have no idea of the total number of rooms each had … My father was the head of a clan in Hosaena as well as the lord of a realm. Not only that, once he was also one of the ten richest men in Ethiopia.'

'Then why are you here? That, too, with an American? Working in a third-rate bar as a waitress? I just don't get it.'

She smiled wryly. A smile that gave away a sense of loathing for the self and also a trace of self-pity.

'Working in a bar was just time-pass. It was a place where I could meet the people of my clan and have open conversations with them. We belong to the Hadiya clan that constitutes just two per cent of the population of Ethiopia. The two major clans in Ethiopia are Amhara and Oromo, which together constitute thirty per cent of the population. They rule Ethiopia today. But we Hadiyas ruled Ethiopia once. Queen Eleni, the famous ruler of Ethiopia in the sixteenth century, belonged to our clan. I was named Eleni Hadiya Sassy because my clan believes that I am the descendant of that queen.'

She paused. She picked up the bottle to pour the next drink. I took my glass away. But she insisted. She made me put my glass back on the table. She poured two stiff drinks. Her eyes were turning red.

'Revenge wars between clans are the curse of Africa. If wealth were divided equally, no child in Africa would go hungry. But every clan wants to control all the wealth and the power. Caught up in all this, they do not see the people who are looting the wealth of Africa. I can say with conviction that when I was young, not a single child of our forty thousand workers ever died of starvation. That was also the mistake that my father made. The eyes of the other clans were on the rich, fertile land on the banks of the Gihon and our coffee plantations, which are what saved our people from starvation. When I say that we, the Hadiyas, owned forty-four per cent of the total coffee produced in Ethiopia, you can imagine the kind of prosperity that I am talking about. The people of the eighth province, the Amhara and Oromo clans, who were systematically doing away with fertile land and leaving barren deserts behind them, drove us away from our lands and our prosperity using the might of their number.'

Suddenly, Kevin opened the door and walked in. The story ended abruptly.

'It's been a long time,' Kevin said. I just smiled.

'You guys sit. I need to get ready to travel. An emergency deputation to Diego Garcia. There's a cargo plane waiting for me.' He went inside to pack his bag.

Rose went in to help him. In about ten minutes, Kevin was ready to leave.

'This is how an officer's life is. Full of uncertainties.' Kevin and Rose kissed goodbye. After that, I did not feel like extending my stay. Though Kevin insisted that I stay on and though I wanted to hear the rest of the story of Eleni Hadiya, I left along with him.

'Did she tell her African stories to you too?' Kevin asked when we were in the elevator. I lowered my head.

'Don't believe a word of it. You can sympathize a bit if you want. Those stories are the kind of hallucinations that take over your mind when you have suffered from starvation for long. Her truth is lifelong poverty and hunger.'

I stared at Kevin in disbelief. He shook his head as though to reconfirm everything he had said.

'If you handle her carefully, you will not lose money,' Kevin said, which sounded almost like a warning.

Lying blackie! You are really an African bitch. You were plotting to tell me stories of wealth to rob me of mine, weren't you? These people are good at this. I was lucky to escape. I thanked God for sending Kevin to the apartment at that moment. My esteem for Kevin went up for putting up with such a poverty-stricken person and providing for her as his own.

After that, though she called a couple of times, I did not answer. There's no saying what kind of web she was weaving. Why take on unnecessary problems? One day, I met a few of her friends at a shopping mall. When they told me that she was upset that I was not answering her calls, the Thomas Chandy in me too became upset. After all, wasn't it hunger and poverty that had reduced her to this? If not, would she go through all this drama? I felt sorry for her. After much thought, I decided to go over to her apartment. Before setting out, I resolved firmly that I would not believe anything that she said any more and that I would protect myself from being the victim of any kind of fraud.

When I got there, she was sitting by herself, sipping a drink. The almost-empty bottle and her red eyes told me that she'd been drinking for a while.

Hmm. It's all free, right. You can afford to drink, you blackie, I thought to myself. This African spider will leave only after it sucks the life out of Kevin.

'Do you still remember the way to this place?' she asked a tad sarcastically. I made up a lot of excuses for not being able to answer the phone and not being able to drop in. She acted as though she believed it all. She poured me a large drink in spite of my saying that I didn't want one. 'Have a drink, man. What if we can never sit together again and have a drink?'

After the second drink, I decided to test her. 'Eleni, you had said that the Amhara and Oromo clans drove you away from your lands and your prosperity. Can an entire clan be just driven away like that? Did you not resist? Did you not think that you were going to be pushed into poverty?'

'They were trying to do this for years, by strengthening their hold on the administration of Addis Ababa. Though we were a minority, they could not do anything until the end of the eighties. But in the early nineties, they latched on to an opportunity. It was then that the Eritrean revolution started heating up in Ethiopia. In 1993, when Eritrea became an independent nation, we, the Hadiyas, became the most hated clan in Ethiopia. We were accused of secretly supporting the Eritrean revolution. We were labelled anti-nationalists. We started being attacked across the country. Using this as their chance, they struck and seized our lands. They beat us up and chased us away. Even as they nailed the blame on an innocent clan, the fact remained that it was exactly what Addis Ababa wanted. Our resistance was weak. I lost my father and my four brothers.'

For the first time, I saw Eleni Hadiya Sassy alias Rose Williams' eyes well up with tears. I poured her a drink. She gulped it down. I poured myself a double and took a sip.

'Does Kevin know all this?' I asked innocently.

'Yes. He knows everything.'

'I respect his largeheartedness.'

'Pah! Largeheartedness!' She spat on the carpet. 'Do you think a Yankee like him will take in an African negro like me without an eye on something?'

'How on earth will he benefit by taking in an African negro like you who's become a nomad after losing her land

and her home? Don't be so thankless.' I decided not to give in.

She glared at me and got up from the sofa. She was a bit wobbly on her feet. She swayed her way to the bedroom. In a short while, she returned with a very large suitcase, which was obviously too heavy for her to lift. She placed that on the teapoy in front of me. All of a sudden, she took out a handgun from under the cushion of the sofa, pointed it in my direction and ordered me to open the suitcase. Scared, I obeyed. I was shocked. That suitcase was full of gold coins and jewellery. I could not even gauge how many kilograms of gold there were in the suitcase.

'You've heard that Ethiopia is a starving country, and we all live in abject poverty. However, this is only a small fraction of my savings. So, now you can imagine how much I am worth. You guys are not intelligent enough to understand that. But a Yankee who landed in Djibouti was.'

She made me close the suitcase, put it back in the room herself, came back, washed her face at the washbasin, wiped her face with a towel and sat down again on the sofa.

'My brother and I, who managed to escape during the civil war, somehow crossed over to our neighbouring country, Djibouti, and began living there quietly. I met Kevin in a bar close to the new naval base set up by America. We knew that our enemies were behind us. They believed strongly that if they did away with my family, the whole Hadiya clan would become extinct. Kevin Peter is just a way of staying alive for the time being. Life with a naval officer who keeps shifting from one base to another is a far more secure way to remain alive than to stay on in Djibouti. They do not have it in them to barge into an American naval officer's house and kill me. If they do, let them come.' She pulled out the gun from under the cushion of the sofa and pointed it at me again. I was frightened. If her unsteady finger squeezed the trigger accidentally … I pleaded with her to put the gun away. She burst out laughing, poured another drink and said, 'My brother is fighting a case in Djibouti to recover everything that we lost. If we win that case, Kevin knows who I will become. So, until the verdict comes out, Kevin will stick with me. Until then, even I need a safe haven. That's all that there is between us. Just that.'

I sat there, caught between belief and disbelief, unable to say anything.

'Why don't you leave now? I'd like to be alone,' she said.

'I'll go. But you have still not told me the meaning of that celebration.'

'It was on the twenty-first of May that Queen Eleni ascended the throne. Everyone dreams that the good old days will return.'

I got up, a bit unsteady on my feet. Like a waitress in a bar, she helped me get to the door.

'Why did you tell me all this? What if I reach out to your enemies and betray you?'

She laughed out loud as though she had heard a big joke. 'There is an old adage in our land – a lizard knows the tree it climbs.'

I did not say anything. As I was putting on my shoes outside the door, she smiled and said, 'When you betray me, tell my foes that I am in Italy.'

I looked at her, surprised. 'I am leaving, TCN. Next week, as soon as Kevin comes back. He has been transferred there.' I suddenly felt a jab of pain. The pain one feels when a loved one goes away.

'I hope the ambitions of your clan will be realized someday.' I bowed. And then I turned and walked away.

Eleni Hadiya Sassy. Will you ever become the queen of Ethiopia? Even if you do, will I ever know of it in another corner of the world? Maybe I will. Like the lizard knows its tree.

The Stones of Gazan

THE STORY FROM THE PAST

The fort of Jerusalem has eight gates – Damascus, Herod, Zion, Jaffa … Of these, the most prominent eastern one is called the Golden Gate. It is believed that Jesus, along with his disciples, came into the city through this gate on Palm Sunday. This gate was closed by the crusaders when they conquered Jerusalem during the last leg of the ninth century. A millennium later, the gate still remains closed. Christians believe that Christ, in his second coming, will break this gate down and enter the city once again; the Jews believe that the Messiah will walk through the gate one day.

It is believed that as a priest, the Messiah would never walk across a cemetery. So, to prevent the Messiah from coming, and even if he does, to prevent him from entering the city, the Muslims of Israel built a cemetery next to the gate. This is proof enough of how deep religious hatred runs in the Middle East.

On the east end of this cemetery, on the western slope of the Mount of Olives, there is also a Christian cemetery, where people have been buried in the hope that they will all rise seeing the second coming of Christ. Different people, different beliefs.

THE STORY FROM THE PRESENT

1

My first visit to the big cemetery next to the garden of Gethsemane in the valley of the Mount of Olives was during Lent, on a Sunday devoted to remembering the dead. When I heard the story of the graves that lay all over without any order, I felt like calling it the jungle of faith and revenge. I mentioned this to Gazan as well. He just smiled, probably because of the layers of meaning that lay within.

2

I met Gazan not so long ago in the lobby of the hotel that I worked for. It was on a cold morning when I was leaving after my night shift and he was waiting for his tourists to turn up. After many a chat on the lobby sofa, I invited Gazan to have a cup of hot coffee in my room. From my small room near the parking area, we could see the hotel's assembly point clearly. This saved him the trouble of having to get up at periodic intervals and leave to check if all his guests had arrived.

And thus, Gazan started to join me for coffee regularly. In a few days, Ahmed also started joining him in my room for coffee. Ahmed was the driver of Gazan's tourist vehicle.

3

They would leave with the tourists at nine in the morning and come back only when the mist started covering the hills of Jerusalem in the evening. By then, I would have woken up for night duty. Come to think of it, I have rarely been awake to see regular days in Israel. For me, Jerusalem was only the distant outline of the Dome of the Rock, the Al-Aqsa Mosque and the many cupolas bathed in neon light. Beyond this, I have not seen Jerusalem.

4

I landed here three years ago thanks to a pilgrim visa that I got through an agency in Mumbai. I had to pay them two lakh rupees for it. Now, neither did I have a visa nor did I have a residence permit. If I were to get caught one day, deportation was certain. The money paid to the agency would then go right down the drain. Israel was one place where people who had the stomach to be illegal immigrants landed up. One could manage to do some work or the other until one got caught. Especially jobs in hotels. This place guaranteed a better pay than you could get anywhere else in the world. Most of the people who worked with me were sardar jis, who had the courage to face anything that came their way.

Vijayettan, who worked with me in a hotel in Tiberias, called people like me, who could be caught at any point in time for working without a visa or any other valid documents, people with the 'Hanuman visa'. I liked its inherent humour. There were so many Malayalis and Punjabis with the Hanuman visa in Jerusalem. The authorities too knew that they needed third-world citizens to clean tables, make the beds and take out the garbage of the privileged. Yet, one could be sure of periodic raids. Because there weren't enough takers for these jobs, the hotel owners would also turn a blind eye to the absence of papers. It was to avoid getting caught that we mostly opted for night shifts. The day shifts were handled by young Palestinians. I have a diploma in hotel management. And I also have the experience of working at a five-star hotel in Kuwait for five years. But…

I've heard that working in Tel Aviv or Eilat would fetch twice as much as what I was earning in Jerusalem. But since that would mean working right under the noses of the authorities, there was no saying when you could get caught. But Jerusalem was not all that much of a problem. Because there was a constant flow of pilgrims, it was difficult to trace people who were living in hiding. Most of the Punjabis who worked with me had already obtained their visas. I wonder when I would cease to be a Hanuman.

5

I've always felt that Gazan was born with all the characteristic traits essential for a guide: the skill of shepherding hundreds of people together, the patience and the tolerance required to handle such a diverse group of people, and the ability to keep entertaining them verbally without boring them one bit. Why, he would start telling a story even as he walked into the room – it might have been about a suicide bombing that happened in Gaza the other day, or the evacuation drama that was unfolding on the West Bank, or the resistance of the Palestinian youth…

Gazan would talk as much about politics as possible to the tourists whom he accompanied. So much so that he had already received two warnings from the Jewish authorities. But speaking about Palestine and her sorrows had become second nature to Gazan.

Ahmed, on the other hand, was not into talking too much. During Gazan's long discourses over coffee, Ahmed would sit and play his favourite game Bantumi on the mobile phone, as though he were not even listening. I've often wondered how there could be a Palestinian who did not react to anything.

Gazan used to say: 'Everyone listens to news from this part of the world with only one ear. Our voices very often fall on deaf ears. Which is why one always feels that we are the only ones to blame. Joji, at least you should listen carefully to what I say. You should go back to your India and tell all this to them. Will you, who came from independent India, understand the trauma of living as a second-class citizen in one's own country?'

6

One day, as I was walking through the narrow street of Via Dolorosa (the way of the cross), a wayside merchant invited me into his shop. He offered me crosses, framed images and figurines at prices that he claimed would be lower than in any other shop. He probably had mistaken me for a pilgrim. He tempted me with a packet containing holy water, holy earth, holy frankincense and holy wine for a mere three shekels. I smiled to myself – add the word 'holy' to anything in Israel and you could sell it like hot cake. Realizing that I was not interested in anything, he pushed a Bible into my hand. 'I don't want anything. This is free,' he said. I accepted it without any shame. It was a Hebrew Bible.

Because I had worked for five years in Kuwait, I understood the Arabic that Gazan and Ahmed spoke, as well as Malayalam. My knowledge of this language was definitely one reason why we bonded so well. But this Hebrew of the Jews – it was a language that one could not master despite repeated attempts. In fact, I wondered how many Jews here knew Hebrew. How did Hebrew matter for people who had come here from America and Europe? Yet, the authorities were trying hard to keep the language alive. Hebrew was now a compulsory language in all the schools. They hoped that over the next ten years, everyone in Israel would know Hebrew. In fact, they had started saying that people who didn't know Hebrew by then would be enemies of the country.

People from different cultures and beliefs can live together well. But people who speak different languages … It was not faith and custom that created the great wall between Palestine and Israel; it was Hebrew and Arabic.

7

One day, Gazan told me the story of the cemetery in the valley of the Mount of Olives, where his grandfather was buried. This was before the mass migration of Jews began at the onset of the First World War. In those days, burying the dead there was easy and widespread. 'But slowly, as Jerusalem fell into the hands of migrants, we lost that hope too. Every Palestinian desired to be buried near the eastern gate of the fort of Jerusalem. In fact, that was an integral part of his belief about his next life. But the Jewish administration saw it as an affront to their belief. That was how, we, Palestinian Christians, who form just one per cent of the population, came to hate the Jews, along with the Muslims.'

Ahmed, who had suddenly snapped out of his game, said, 'It was definitely with a motive of revenge that we insisted that the tombs of Yasin Malik and Yasser Arafat be in Jerusalem itself. But they did not agree. However, more Palestinian tombs will surely rise near the eastern gate of the Jerusalem fort. Let their Messiah come stomping over the bodies of our dead brothers.' And then, Ahmed went back to his Bantumi as though nothing had happened.

8

When Gazan told me that it was All Souls' Day, when the dead were remembered, I thought of my grandparents who were laid to rest in the cemetery of the Arthat Valiya Pally in Kunnamkulam. Suddenly, the smell, taste and texture of local mangoes, water apples and jackfruit, which they used to save for Jojimon, assailed my senses. Though their lives revolved entirely in and around the small village of Kunnamkulam, the unlimited love that filled their large hearts always amazed me.

'This day is loved more than Christmas or Easter by the Christians of Palestine, and it brings in hordes of tourists. After all, this is an opportunity to see all your loved ones who are with God now. We are people who'd love to visit the graves of our loved ones every single day of the year.

But we will be stopped at the checkpoint. And then there would be a hundred questions. Why are you going to Jerusalem? What's your job? To destroy which building have they sent you here? How many Jews have you been ordered to kill? These questions really get to you, Joji. Just imagine explaining why you want to visit the land of your forefathers to some foreigner who is a Jewish immigrant from Poland, Russia or Turkey! But you have to patiently answer all the questions. If not, a Palestinian will be sent back without the permission to enter Jerusalem. This is the only day on which we can walk in freely, which is why we love this day so much. I am not talking about myself, Joji. Though it can be cancelled at any point of time, I have a guide licence. That is the only reason why I can come and go as I please. But this is not the fate of an ordinary Palestinian who is surrounded by Jews on all four sides. Forget stepping into Jerusalem, they do not like Palestinians even looking in that direction. That is why they are building such a high wall to cordon off Palestine.'

'Gazan, they can raise it as high as they want to. But they are only going to realize that it can never ever be higher than the self-respect of the Palestinian!' Ahmed exclaimed, as though, all of a sudden, he had woken up again.

9

By the time we got there, the cemetery was overflowing. Armed Israeli soldiers were constantly doing their rounds.

They allowed me to enter without searching me. But they stopped Gazan. He was allowed to enter only after he showed them a sheaf of papers. As he looked at the graves, Gazan said, 'No Palestinian, including myself, is a citizen of Israel. All we have are resident permits – only the right to stay. If your country can't accommodate us, all we ask for is an independent nation unto ourselves. Is that wrong, Joji? Why is the world punishing us so much for that?'

I did not have an answer.

We started cleaning the tombstones of our loved ones and decorating them with flowers. Gazan and I cleaned the tombstone of his grandfather as well. We lit candles. And then, for a while, he stood with his eyes closed in prayer. Before we turned to leave, Gazan placed a stone on top of the grave. Seeing my curious look, Gazan explained: 'This is a custom amongst us. Whenever we visit the graves of our loved ones, we will place a stone on top of each of the graves.' I looked at the other graves. All of them had two or three stones on top of them. 'This is how we figure out how many people visited our loved ones across a year. The new year of the dead starts today. We start counting afresh from today. A long time ago, there would be up to one hundred stones on my grandfather's grave. Graves without stones are an insult to our community. Today, you will not find more than ten or fifteen stones on any grave. Who will come? We have let go of our loved ones fearing the roving eyes of the Jews. Everyone is tired of this imprisoned life.'

We walked back to the hotel through the centuries-old narrow streets of Jerusalem, in total silence.

10

How many Malayalis are there in Israel? Is asking this question as meaningless as asking how many Mathais there are in Kottayam? I've heard that there are a number of Carmelite priests and nuns in Israel. They are cloistered within the four walls of the monastery, praying and fasting. Then there are the Hanuman visa guys like Vijayettan and I – probably a few hundred like that. Most of them are hotel employees – none holding high office. There were always lucky Jews who had immigrated from America or Europe for those jobs. As Ahmed would put it: 'The locusts who came to destroy the yield of Israel.'

Ahmed used to say, 'Look Gazan, they will feed off this land and then, after sucking it dry, move on to some other country. Once our resources have all dried up, they will not want to stay on in this country for the sake of any religion or belief. What relationship do they have with this land anyway? They keep landing up here expecting the good life that the Jewish government keeps promising them. But is that the reality for you and me? Isn't this the soil in which our umbilical cords are buried? Why else are we putting up with all this hardship even when the wealth of Arabia keeps beckoning?'

I suddenly remembered the Jews that migrated out of Mattancherry. Where would they be now? It would not be easy to locate even one of them. They were always an integral part of this culture. Yet, I would hope, hopelessly, that I'd unexpectedly bump into one of them on a street in Israel, and that he would sponsor me and end all my visa problems. At the end of the day, it is to our newest angsts that we tag our biggest dreams.

11

On the days we met, Gazan would call me 'Bombay Bhai'. He used to speak with great pride about Indira Gandhi. He'd reminisce how during her times, India was a great friend of Palestine, Abu Arafat and the Arabs. He knew Amitabh Bachchan, Dharmendra and *Sholay*. He did not know the new films, heroes, and the heads of state. My India was the India of the sixties and the seventies that showered love on the international community. For the Arabs, the Afghans and the Iraqis, who thirsted for freedom, the India of those times, with her non-aligned stance, was in itself, a world filled with expectation and hope. Why did India's heart shrivel up after that without a trace of warmth or tenderness?

12

One morning, Gazan came to my room with a stone. 'Joji, you do nothing but sleep most of the day. If you don't mind, could you please go to the Mount of Olives, place this stone on my grandfather's grave and tell him that it was sent by his beloved grandson Gazan?'

I accepted the assignment happily.

Soon it became a regular practice. Very often, when he came in the morning, Gazan would have a few stones in his bag. He would take each one out, place it on the table and say, 'This was sent by my father, this was sent by my fourth aunt's second son, this is from my elder sister's grandson, Thahira, this is from my uncle's daughter Rubaine … Please place all these on the grave and tell my grandfather how sad we are that we could not come ourselves.'

I found all this amusing. After placing all the stones, I would wander around in the cemetery. I would count how many stones were placed on each grave. After I started going to the cemetery, there were more stones on Gazan's grandfather's grave than on anyone else's. When Gazan heard this, I saw pride bloom on his face like a flower. 'Joji, everyone at home is really fond of you. They would like to meet you. You should come home with me one day.'

'I will,' I said. But I was never able to fulfil that promise.

13

One day, Ahmed came into the room in a rage, yelling at Gazan. I have never heard Ahmed raise his voice like that. His face was red with anger.

'If you meet that girl again, I will stop working with you. I have nothing more to say.'

'Ahmed, you don't know anything. Had it not been for her, my guide licence would not have been renewed. She has promised to help us further.'

'You must be a dog to go after the crumbs of help that a Jew throws your way.'

'You are mistaken. She empathizes with us. I understood that over time.'

'You should have told her clearly that a Palestinian does not need her empathy.'

'Why on earth is she to blame for all the terrible things that the mad Jewish government is doing?'

'Joji, look at how he sympathizes with a Jew. Dogs. They can never be trusted. Every Christian has a leaning towards a Jew. And yet, you keep bleating about all the pain and the hardships that you suffered in the past. But none of you think even once of what we are going through today.'

'Ahmed, don't simply...'

Ahmed walked out of the room, furious.

Gazan looked at me and smiled.

'It's okay, Joji. Ahmed is mad. He is hopping mad just because a kind Jewish girl offered to help us.'

I forgot to enquire further about this incident; I did not even ask the girl's name. That was because I was all worked up after my sister called to inform me that Appa had been admitted to Lisie Hospital as his blood pressure had shot up. Gazan probably sensed this, because he, too, did not open up the conversation again.

14

It was one of my all-time wishes to visit the Church of the Nativity in Bethlehem. When I shared with Gazan my angst over not having the relevant documents to visit Palestine, he gave me confidence, hope and promise. But the promise stayed unfulfilled for a long time. When I was almost sure that Gazan had forgotten about the promise, he came into my room in a great hurry one morning and asked me to get ready to go to Bethlehem. Though I was a bit flustered, I got ready immediately. A tour group from Lithuania was staying in our hotel. Along with them, I, too, boarded the bus and occupied the rear seat. They must have thought that I was an employee of the tour company or the guide's assistant. Gazan explained the sights en route in great detail. It was on that day that I realized how beautifully he could tell stories.

This journey, that circled the valley of the Jerusalem mountains to climb 750 metres above sea level to reach Bethlehem, was the best experience I had in my life in Israel. But on the way back, the bus was stopped near the great wall that divided Israel and Palestine. A military officer with a gun stepped into the bus and asked everyone to hold up their passports and travel permits. My heart skipped a beat. The officer started inspecting the documents. Finally, when it was my turn, Gazan came over and spoke to the officer. I could not make out what was happening. 'I told him that your passport and documents are stuck in the luggage compartment. He agreed because you are a foreigner. A Palestinian will never walk so freely away from this wall.'

15

The next day, Ahmed came alone to my room.

'Where's Gazan?' I asked.

'I gave up the job in his vehicle.'

'What happened, Ahmed?'

'Did he tell you anything about that girl?' Ahmed asked.

'No. But I don't think it is anything like what you suspect,' I said, trying to defend Gazan.

'Joji, you know nothing about the games these Jews play. She's a spy. She's just using Gazan to know more about us. I'm just upset that he does not see through all this, despite his day-long pro-Palestine rhetoric. I can easily guess what is going to happen between the two of them. If something like that happens, you just tell him, Joji, that she will meet the same fate as her parents did.'

There were a few stones on my table that Gazan had left with me the previous day. Ahmed saw them as he was leaving. He picked up one stone and played with it scornfully. And then, very unexpectedly, in a mad frenzy, he hurled the stone at the wall. It broke the mirror next to the window.

'He gifts these stones to dead people and graves. But we use the same stones to stay alive. This is the last line of our defense.'

Ahmed left my room like a howling dervish.

16

When I saw Gazan next, I told him about Ahmed's visit. It was then that Gazan told me all about Vivian Frank, the Jew.

Vivian and her family were from Algeria. Her parents were no more. She was brought up by her old grandparents. And they were street performers who played the violin in Paternoster Square to eke out a living. Occasionally, Vivian also used to go along with them to play the violin. That's how they met. Vivian still spoke sadly about the days when she was in Europe for her higher studies and had to play the violin on trains to England, Germany and Hungary to buy food for herself. She was lucky enough to find a job recently in the Ministry of External Affairs. 'I told Ahmed that this posting would help us – and that is why he is upset and angry with me. Do you know Joji, Vivi's parents were killed in a suicide bombing in Gaza the year they moved here. Yet, she has no animosity towards Palestinians. Not just that, she also understands and empathizes with our situation. It was this that drew me closer to her.'

'But what Ahmed says…'

'I know. Seeing everyone as an enemy is a disease. His condition will go from bad to worse and he will end up in the Hamas suicide squad.'

Suddenly, Ahmed's warning struck me like lightning. But I was scared to tell Gazan about it.

17

Saturday was the Shabbat of the Jews. It was a public holiday. Schools and government offices would be closed. The shops of orthodox Jews would remain shut. Why, in areas where only Jews lived, even driving was not allowed. But it was a very busy day for us. By Friday evening, the Jews would come in droves to hotels. And then, until way past midnight, food and wine and hymns and psalms would flow. This singing, with rhythmic clapping and occasional ululation, is the most beautiful music I've ever heard. I doubt if there is any other clan that ushers the Holy Shabbat with so much joy.

That day was a first Shabbat. For Jews, the first Shabbat after marriage is celebrated with even greater pomp than the wedding. They invite their relatives and friends and throw a big feast. They sing love songs to the bride and the groom. These days, this event takes place in hotels. Wine for the asking, food for the asking – we waiters would break our backs from running up and down endlessly.

By morning, I was really exhausted. I just fell into bed as soon as I reached the room. I did not even feel like having a cup of tea. I woke up only around four in the evening. There were signs of Gazan having come and gone. There was a cup of cold tea on the table that he had probably made for me to drink when I woke up. Next to it, there was a stone. And along with it, a note. '*Joji, when you have the time, please keep this stone on my grandfather's grave. From someone who really wants to be his granddaughter. I will tell you everything in person.*'

I felt that Ahmed's doubts were coming true. Gazan and Vivian Frank ... I was scared. I decided that I would tell Gazan about Ahmed's threat.

The next day as well as the day after that, I waited for Gazan to turn up. He did not come. The wait went on for weeks and then months. But my room never hosted Gazan ever again. I asked everyone I knew; nobody knew anything. I tried calling him on his mobile; it was always switched off. I never saw Ahmed too after that. Between the giant walls of Israel and Palestine, where could I go looking for them? My heart burns when I think of them. God, what on earth could have happened between them?

Gulam Hussain

It was when I was sitting in a restaurant in the ancient Irani market in Doha, entertaining myself by blowing clouds of apple-flavoured-hookah smoke, that I saw a strangely dressed old man walk through the street.

Right then, Al Jazeera was breaking the news that the Lebanese prime minister had resigned in Saudi Arabia. The Arabs seated around me with their hookahs started to talk about this anxiously and voiced their worry about the political repercussions this could have in the Middle East. A few of them critiqued the lack of intelligence of Arab leaders loudly. A few were angry and upset about their own helplessness. A few spoke of leaving all this behind and relocating to Europe the very next day if possible. And some others, predicting that another war would break out immediately, abandoned their food and their hookahs and ran to the grocery store to stock up on essentials. On the whole, the environment was high-strung.

It was then that the old man walked past us on the street, dragging his foot, as though none of these things would impact him in any way. His ash-coloured beard, round hat and sparkling eyes reminded me of the old, wise men in movies based on the Old Testament. He was looking around carefully as he walked, as though he were searching for something that he had lost. Beneath the tables in the restaurant, the trash can on the wayside, in between the boxes stacked in the toy shop, underneath the car that was parked – he peered and poked at everything in his quest.

'Hello Chacha, aaj kuch mila?' the bearer in the restaurant asked the old man as he poured steaming hot kahwah into my cup.

He stopped searching for a minute and turned around with great difficulty. He then uttered a loud cuss word in Hindi and walked away. The bearer laughed out loud as though he'd asked the question just to provoke the old man.

'What is he searching for?' I asked, unable to contain my curiosity.

'A tiger cub.'

'What?'

'Tiger cub!'

I did not get it. I even wondered for a split second if he was pulling my leg. The bearer moved away from my curiosity to the next table. I looked expectantly at the people around me, but engrossed as they were in their high-strung political debate, they ignored me altogether.

An Arab city, an old man, a tiger cub – these three unrelated things remained undigested with me as I walked back home after my meal.

A few days later, I went to meet a sheikh in his majlis to discuss the possibility of a partnership in a business enterprise I was planning to start shortly. The majlis was away from the palace, adjacent to the air-conditioned royal stable that could accommodate up to four hundred horses. This compound also contained wide, green walkways for the horses, as well as the quarters for the staff. The majlis, with its hanging lamps from Turkey, carpets from Iran and paintings from Europe, looked more royal than the palace. Even as we discussed business, I could not help but keep glancing at one particular wall that was filled with black-and-white photographs in frames. It was on that day that I realized that black-and-white photographs are so much more beautiful than colour photographs. The talent of an unknown artist was very evident in the way the frames had been composed.

While we drank tea following the discussion, I spent some time taking a closer look at these images. Many of them captured a young man speeding by on a horse. A few captured him accepting trophies and walking down mud roads. Then there were images of the same young man with lions, leopards, tigers, elephants and giraffes.

'These are images of my father. He really loved animals,' the sheikh said with great pride in his voice.

He had walked over, seeing my interest in the photographs. As I was about to turn away, one picture caught my eye. The youth in it resembled the younger, full-of-life form of the old man that I had seen on the street. This image was placed prominently in the centre of the wall. But before I could ask the sheikh anything, other guests arrived, and I had to leave in a hurry.

A few days later, I went to a distant labour camp to meet two of my old classmates whom I hadn't seen in ages. As we sat devouring pomegranates, roasted peanuts and the local news, the old man, for some reason, surfaced in our conversation.

'Ah! Anyone who goes to the Irani market will definitely see him. He has been there for so many years – long before all of us arrived here.'

'Is he an Indian?' I asked.

'No! Not at all. He is an Iranian. He speaks Hindi very well.'

'They say he wanders all around searching for a…'

'Yes, a tiger cub.'

'The bearer at the restaurant said the same thing. A tiger cub! That, too, in a big city like this? You're mad.'

'No, it's not madness. It's the truth. He's been searching for the last twenty years. Poor guy.'

'An old Iranian, an Arab city, a tiger cub, a search that has been going on for twenty years … the pieces just don't fit,' I said.

'Yes, it's a long story. There's one man who knows him and his stories very well in this camp: Ansari. He will be able to put all the pieces of this puzzle together.'

We set out to find Ansari at once. We found him in the large kitchen of the labour camp. It had been over five years that Ansari had joined as the chef's assistant.

'The name of that old man is Gulam Hussain,' Ansari began, seated on one of the steps leading to the kitchen. 'His connection with India started a long time ago when he went to Pune to study engineering. But halfway into the programme, he had to go back – all because one monsoon, he decided to make the hostel a home for a stray dog. This created an uproar. Though the majority of the students and teachers appreciated the gesture, there was a small group who was against this. In the meantime, an English newspaper carried a picture of Gulam Hussain with the dog in his hand, in an article titled, "An Animal Lover from Iran". This caused a stir in Iran as well, since he had violated religious dictates with the abominable act of raising a dog in India. This was the time when the Iranian revolution was unfolding under the leadership of Khomeini. The time when traditional customs were followed very strictly, and everyone kept an eye on the other person to ensure that there were no aberrations. The time when even small mistakes were not forgiven. Khomeini's revolutionaries turned against the family of Gulam Hussain. The government passed an order that he be summoned back to Iran immediately. But he was not willing to throw himself at the mercy of those religious fanatics. Gulam Hussain, who said he was going back to Iran, surfaced next in Kenya. And from there, he procured a Bachelor's degree and a Master's degree in zoology, as well as a few other qualifications. All of which led to him getting a job in the Kenyan forest department.

'It was then that a sheikh from here, along with his entourage, went to Kenya for a jungle safari. Because they were the special guests of the government, Gulam Hussain was entrusted with the task of accompanying them. It was during the long eight-day journey through the jungle that the sheikh realized the deep bond that Gulam had with the wild animals. Lions with fresh blood on their lips would put their paws on his shoulders playfully; crouching tigers would walk behind him like docile dogs; wild elephants that came charging would move aside when they heard his admonitions; warring wolves wagged their tails in his presence.

'After the jungle safari, the sheikh was seized with a desire to set up a small zoo in his city that would have lions and tigers and leopards and every animal that roamed free in the jungle. The zookeeper would be none other than Gulam Hussain. But Gulam Hussain rejected the idea summarily. Animals should live in their natural ecosystem. The desert had camels, gazelles and sand cats. There was no need to ship poor creatures that did not belong to the desert there.

'But the sheikh was determined. He went back and spent a fortune to create a garden in the heart of his city. He planted trees to simulate a forest. He invested in climate control. Then he brought elephants and tigers from India, lions, leopards and giraffes from Africa, and rare, exotic birds from different parts of the world.

'The sheikh then went back to Kenya to request Gulam Hussain to be his zookeeper. This time, Gulam found it difficult to reject the request, because it came more as an order routed through the Kenyan government. The order stated clearly that if he did not honour the request of a friend of the Kenyan government, he would not only lose his job but also be deported. Losing his job would not have been a problem for him, but having to go back to Iran was unthinkable. It was in this way that Gulam Hussain, the Iranian youth, landed up in the Arab city of Doha.'

As he was telling the story, Ansari served us hot chapatis and dal fry. We sat in the clean hall adjacent to the kitchen and ate. He then gave us black tea with mint. Tea in hand, we walked to Ansari's room. As we sipped the steaming hot tea, Ansari told us the rest of the story.

'Before Gulam Hussain arrived, about ten to twenty of us who had experience working in different zoos in India had already reached here. I, myself, had had twelve years of experience working in the Trivandrum Zoo. But when Gulam Hussain stepped in, the entire routine changed. He had his own jungle-ways of feeding, bathing and taking care of the animals, none of which fitted into our regimented way of doing things. Slowly, a conflict grew between us. We started disobeying him. This enraged him even more. He inflicted all kinds of punishments on us. We took out the anger we had towards him on the animals – all of which he promptly discovered. His story was that every single animal in the zoo spoke to him. I have no clue how true this was. But every animal responded positively to him when he called out their names, which revealed the love and the bond between them. And this made us really jealous – we had to poke these animals with sticks, beat them with belts, and scare them with loud sounds to make them obey.

'One day, a huge quarrel broke out between Gulam Hussain and a few of us about the meat that had been fed to a lion. He was not ready to make even the slightest compromise when it came to feeding the animals. He reported the matter to the sheikh, and a few of us were sent back home the same night. Knowing that the same fate awaited the rest of us, we ganged up and plotted to somehow oust Gulam Hussain from the zoo.

'So, one day, when Gulam Hussain went for his morning walk, we released a few animals from their cages. With the doors to the world thrown open, though the animals stood confused without the iron bars around them for a while, they soon ran out on to the street. It was the hour when people were going to work in the morning. They screamed in fear when they unexpectedly saw wild animals on the road. They honked, shouted, and pelted stones to drive them away. The distressed animals ran across the highway, the park and the shopping mall. In a few seconds, city-life was totally disrupted.

'Because many people were not aware of a private zoo in the midst of the city, most of them could not fathom where the animals had come from. Some of them even thought that an enemy nation had attacked them by releasing wild animals into the city.

'Soon, the police arrived. They came with the order to shoot the animals on sight. But they had no clue where they were hiding. The police, along with the people, started looking for them. A lion that tried to cross the border was shot dead by the army.

'Though the entire city was in turmoil, Gulam Hussain was not aware of anything. He had seen people gather on the street as they do when there is an accident. But he continued with his morning walk since that had nothing to do with him. It was only when he got back that he realized what had happened. The sheikh, literally shivering with rage, had reached the zoo by then. We managed to convince him that it was Gulam Hussain who had released the animals before he went for a walk and that he used to do so regularly. And the sheikh, who had seen Gulam Hussain walking with the animals a number of times during his visits to the zoo, believed what we said.'

At this point in the story, someone ran into our room, breathless. 'Did you know? There is a big problem in Saudi. A few princes have been arrested for corruption. A war will soon break out.'

Ansari's story was interrupted. Everyone rushed to switch on the TV. All the channels were tracking the story that was unfolding. The helicopter in which a prince had tried to escape, had crash-landed at the border. As the news spread, more people from the camp came into the room to find out what was happening. And then it became the venue of a major political debate. As soon as I realized that neither Ansari's story nor I had any relevance there, I said my goodbyes and left. But the man called Gulam Hussain stayed in my mind. The curiosity to know the rest of the story grew within me throughout my journey.

I drove to the Irani market. I went to the same restaurant and sat at the same table from where I had seen Gulam Hussain the other day. It was the same bearer who came to take my order. I started a conversation with him as he was changing the filter of the hookah.

'I heard most of the story of the old Iranian man from someone else. What happened to the animals that went out on to the street that day?'

The bearer made me narrate the story that I had heard. Though there were slight differences between the story I narrated and the story he knew, he told me the rest of it.

'Gulam Hussain stepped out into the street after requesting the sheikh not to be impatient, assuring him that he would bring all the animals out there back into the zoo. He then wandered through the entire city calling each animal by name. Believe it or not, the animals that the people and the police could not find started coming out one after another from amidst parked cars, from behind abandoned boxes, from desolate dark alleys, and started following him like domesticated pets.

'Out of the seventeen animals that escaped, one lion had been shot dead by the army at the border. Gulam found fifteen animals by evening. People watched with fear and amazement as Gulam Hussain led these animals through the streets of the city. After putting them into their cages, he stepped out into the street again. The sixteenth missing animal was a tiger cub. There was no way he could have left the city or stayed in hiding for this long anywhere. But even after repeatedly scouting the entire city over several days, he could not find the cub. The sheikh was also very fond of the cub. He announced a big reward for anyone who could provide information about it. This inspired many labourers to search for the cub late into the night – in fact, this became a regular sight in the city. But it was all in vain. Nobody could find the cub. All this happened twenty years ago. Everyone has forgotten this incident. But Gulam Hussain still roams the streets of this city in search of that animal.'

The bearer concluded his story and was all set to move to the next table.

'Wait, just a moment. What happened to the fifteen animals that he brought back to the zoo? Does that zoo still exist?'

'That zoo was closed immediately after this incident and all the employees were dismissed. But those animals? No idea. Once an animal tries to escape – be it a lion or a tiger – the fate is the same.'

It was then that Al Jazeera released a news flash – another prince who tried to flee the country had also died in a chopper crash.

The bearer abandoned me and went behind the new news story.

At that moment, old Gulam Hussain passed that way. He was still searching for the lost cub. An Arab who was smoking his hookah and was not interested in the news flash asked him something. He just lifted his hand casually and walked away.

As I inhaled the smoke from the apple-flavoured hookah, I wondered about the fate of the lions who had been caught after they broke free.

BENYAMIN is a novelist and short-story writer in Malayalam. His novel *Aadujeevitham*, which has been reprinted more than a hundred times and has sold over two lakh copies, won him the Kerala Sahitya Akademi Award in 2009 and has been translated into many languages. The English translation, *Goat Days*, was shortlisted for the Man Asian Literary Prize and the DSC Prize for South Asian Literature. In 2018, his novel *Jasmine Days* won the JCB Prize for Literature and the Crossword Book Award for fiction in translation. The follow-up to it, *Al Arabian Novel Factory*, was published in 2019. *Body and Blood*, the English translation of his novel *Shareerasastram* was published in 2020.

SWARUP B.R. is an independent brand consultant and one of the founder-directors of Stark Communications Pvt. Ltd, the most awarded advertising agency in South India. His translation of Benyamin's novel *Shareerasastram* was published in 2020 as *Body and Blood*.

30 Years *of*

HarperCollins *Publishers* India

At HarperCollins, we believe in telling the best stories and finding the widest possible readership for our books in every format possible. We started publishing 30 years ago; a great deal has changed since then, but what has remained constant is the passion with which our authors write their books, the love with which readers receive them, and the sheer joy and excitement that we as publishers feel in being a part of the publishing process.

Over the years, we've had the pleasure of publishing some of the finest writing from the subcontinent and around the world, and some of the biggest bestsellers in India's publishing history. Our books and authors have won a phenomenal range of awards, and we ourselves have been named Publisher of the Year the greatest number of times. But nothing has meant more to us than the fact that millions of people have read the books we published, and somewhere, a book of ours might have made a difference.

As we step into our fourth decade, we go back to that one word – a word which has been a driving force for us all these years.

Read.

Harper Collins · 4th · HARPER PERENNIAL · HARPER BUSINESS · HARPER BLACK · हार्पर हिन्दी

HarperCollins *Children's Books* · HARPER DESIGN · HARPER VANTAGE · Harper Sport